Courtesans — Part II

By
Michael Polowetzky

COURTESANS

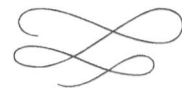

Part II

Mama and her Unlikely Friend

BY

MICHAEL POLOWETZKY

ISBN: 978-1-63950-010-9   [Paperback Edition]
       978-1-63950-011-6   [eBook Edition]

Printed and bound in The United States of America.

Writers Apex

Gateway Towards Success

8063 MADISON AVE #1252
Indianapolis, IN 46227
+13176596889
www.writersapex.com

The world is a closed door, a barrier.
Yet it is also the way through.

Simone Weil (1909-1943)

Part 2

Mama and her Unlikely Friend

DECISION

"NO, NO, STOP! STOP!" Rolande de Montfort heard cry a still, small voice. "Stop!" admonished this inner spirit. One, that if she was yet silent, unseen, was also a phantom grown steadily louder, her call ever more persistent from the time young possessor experienced that mysterious summons in Paris on the Right embankment. "Don't do it, Child!" commanded the inner spirit. "This is not your mission, Child! This is not what you are meant for in life!"

Rolande instantly halted.

Grimaced pondering.

Clinched her fists.

"You're right," she whispered. "You're absolutely right! This kind of life is not really meant for me.

The girl made to flee.

"Brigadier Aslan! Brigadier Aslan!" shouted Rolande, frantically signaling to the driver of a limousine nearby. "Get me, quick!"

The old warrior instantly jumped into the vehicle and came to collect his pensive young charge.

"What's all this about? What's going on?" queried French president Alexander Markovsky, startled. He flummoxed as his just moments earlier loyal companion abruptly pulled free of her protector's arm and stepped away. "Where are you going, my *Sweet Thing*?"

"Not with you, that's for sure, Sandy my boy!" answered Rolande with unaccustomed public confidence. She boldly leaping into an awaiting car. Then, after closing the door safely behind, the girl added through the open window: "I've got some important work to do now! Some critical work which you and your immoral, self-centered, grasping

1

kind will never be able to help me! Goodbye, Sandy! I'm leaving you! And I won't be coming back! Ever!"

"Now, let's get me out of this dreadful place, Brigadier Aslan!" the pretty rebel in short, violet colored dress instructed her driver. "Let's get as far and as fast away from here as we can!"

"At once, Mademoiselle"

"Also, let's exit the *other* way!" insisted Rolande, motioning they avoid once more passing the *Baroque* marble depicting a lustful, middle-aged Pluto carrying off teenage Persephone without the nymph putting up any serious fight. "Let's get out of here, the *other* way around. I do so hate seeing that ghastly statue!"

LETTER

Dearest Mama,

Your Missy needs to go away for a while. She knows it will all be for the best. Don't worry too much about silly President Markovsky. He will get over my leaving. I am confident he will soon find another, more appropriate girl to amuse him. Besides, I'm not at all sure he really cares for redheads. Ultimately, like Elizabeth I, Henry VIII, Charles Darwin, Mary Queen of Scots, Richard the Lion Heart, Garibaldi, Dante Rossetti, Billy the Kid, Charlotte Bronte, Galileo, Vincent Van Gogh, Winston Churchill, Thomas Jefferson, Mark Twain, and James Joyce, we redheads are a bit too independent-minded for his taste.

Your Missy came to realize she will never be a traditional member of our clan. A voice inside tells her so and she must obey. There is no choice! Truly! If Missy's current actions anger or disappoint you, please believe she is terribly sorry. But this must be done! Please also extend my deepest, most sincere apologies to Auntie Philippine, to Aunties Leonie, and to all those others who have loved, nurtured, and protected me since I was a little girl.

I understand my destiny is not located in an upper class garden party holding a powerful man's arm. Where is it found instead? I am not at all sure. However, I will definitely know where it is when I get there.

Does this letter sound addled? I guess it does. That is because I do feel more than a little addled at the moment.

Maybe experiences like this make even the best of us addled!

Anyway, bless you Mama! Bless all those I love (both living and dead)! I will contact you again when I have finally got my head screwed on straight. I will write again when I have finally arrived where I am supposed to be and when I have finally become what destiny wants me to become.

Always yours, Missy

PICTURES AT AN EXHIBITION

"MADEMOISELLE ROLANDE JUST SUDDENLY got up and left me!" moaned President Markovsky, struggling to recount the tale as he wept profusely over Countess Celine de Montfort's comforting left shoulder. "Your daughter just suddenly pulled away her arm from me. She abruptly turned her back on me and left me!"

"There, there, Your Grace."

As on every Thursday evening, this noted couple was secluded in the elegant first floor *Louis XV Style*-salon of Palais Montfort, the hostess's cream color, Baroque, a Parisian mansion located at No. 3. Rue Artemis. If Markovsky was compelled to look ever strong in public, obliged to always speak bold and confident when addressing crowds, the nation's elected leader knew he still remained free to relax and confide his honest thoughts upon retreating to the privacy of his special chum's sheltering arms.

"T*here, there*, Your Grace. I'm here for you now."

Along this hall's four delicately papered walls, above the chamber's waxed, dark oak panel floor, more than five centuries of previous *Montfort Ladies* (several nude) observed the action of their descendent attentively. These ancestors gazed down in judgment upon their tribe's current leader through portraits crafted by artists from Leonardo, Caravaggio, and Rembrandt to Goya, Monet, and Picasso.

"And it all occurred while the German Chancellor, the British Prime Minister and the *UN* Secretary General were all watching!" further blubbered the French president, he now resting his sorrowful face and trembling upper torso against Celine's ample bust and significant cleavage. He was six feet six, the chatelaine, a foot shorter. The unhappy, weeping gent pressing down upon the lady from above was not just groping, lustful, but also heavy.

"*There, there,* Your Grace" soothed Celine. "*There, there.* It's over now. You are now here with me, Your Grace. I will take care of you now."

"Mlle. Rolande told me that she henceforth possesses some kind of special *calling*–she told me about how she from today is given a critical *mission* to *fulfill*," continued the President. He was still describing the personal embarrassment suffered at last afternoon's elite, high-power garden party. It was a political, public relations fiasco captured across Europe on the front page of all the continent's daily, mass-distribution, conservative, lowbrow tabloids.

"It sounds as if Mlle. Rolande has been infected by the mad ideas of that Middle Eastern refugee muralist Pascale Kedari and her leftist followers!" Markovsky wailed. "The followers who want to employ that talented girl and her pictures to bring down our whole society– to entirely replace it with some kind of harebrained socialist nirvana!"

The dejected schemer gave Celine another entitled, proprietary grope.

"I am naturally sorry Mademoiselle. Kedari was assassinated, of course!" voter-pandering Markovsky was studious to add. "The Middle Eastern refugee girl was not even twenty-years old! Even so, you must admit that poor Mademoiselle. Kedari and her crazy left-wing disciples were–*still are*–ultimately just a bunch of dangerous, wild-eyed revolutionaries!"

"*There, there*, Your Grace."

"It seems Mlle. Rolande now wants to be a wild-eyed revolutionary, too!"

"You should never forget that my Rolande–that my little *Missy*– is also a teenager," admonished the young runaway's mother with barely concealed maternal pride. "Teenagers, especially girls, tend to be yearners, romantics, idealists. I certainly was one at that age!– Teenagers, especially girls, are often attracted to what they perceive as noble, lofty issues. Teenagers, especially girls, often want to become part of a cause they view as far greater than themselves. A powerful, grand, deathless movement, crusade, existing long before these insecure, mortal daughters were ever born–one, sure to also exist long after the fragile, wavering kids depart this troubled, disappointing life. I certainly thought and felt that way too, when I was a teenager."

"After all" her parent continued, "keep in mind the books my dreamy, impressionable *Missy* has been reading in the last few months? Ones, about Simone Weil, Jeanne d'Arc, Anne Frank and St. Therese of Lisieux."

Celine halted, reflective.

"Considering my good hearted-*Missy*'s fondness for such uplifting reading material, it should not at all be surprising this girl too decided she possesses a spiritual *calling*–concluded that she too was appointed by the heavens above to fulfill a glorious *mission.*'"

With: high forehead and cheekbones; deep, thoughtful green eyes; a straight nose; good teeth; strong chin; charming painted lips; firm, unblemished rosy skin; sculpted neck; thick, rich cherry blonde locks falling below bare shoulders; fetching young body clothed in a light-colored strapless opera gown–this particular chatelaine appeared far more her daughter's near-lookalike big sister than mother.

"But it occurred in front of all the cameras!" again sobbed Markovsky, he still in need of additional tender, feminine reassurance. "Mlle. Rolande left me in front of all the cameras! People all around Europe must think I'm a fool! They must think I am a blithering idiot! One, who can't even keep his women under control! They must think I now go around with a mad girl!"

"So this hornie scoundrel looks upon my *Little Treasure*, views my own beloved Missy is a *mad girl*?" mused her mother silently with rightful maternal pride. "People once thought Jeanne d'Arc, too, was a *mad girl*! People once thought Simone Weil too, was a *mad girl*!"

"In front of all those cameras!"

"Well, Your Grace has finally learned that he must curb his desire for teenagers," advised Celine, more than a slight measure of reproof detected in her previous reliably supportive counsel. "As every Mama on Earth can tell you, teenagers, especially girls, are quite an unpredictable handful! Anyone thinking teenagers, especially girls, are simple to manage, painless to guide, easy to keep under proper adult supervision, ought to get their head examined!"

She squeezed her doleful partner's right hand tight to display emphasis.

"Yes, yes, now I finally do understand," sniffled Markovsky, at last. If his eyes are remaining red, bleary, he was at last exhausted from weeping self-pity. He soon delivered the long-suffering countess a humble, boyish smile of needy gratitude. "Yes, yes, I understand at last, my precious Celine. I promise I've finally learned my lesson! I will never stray from you again, my dearest, my most faithful, most dependable, most trusted *Sweetheart*. I will from now on want and listen to you, alone! I will look only to you for advice, aid, comfort, solace!" Markovsky grew hesitant.

Squirmed.

Pondered.

Wiped his eyes with a silk, monogrammed handkerchief taken from suit pocket.

"That is of course," the President entreated, "if my all-wise, if my all-knowing original Sweetheart can please, please, please still find it in her noble heart and soul to somehow take me back?'" "

"Oh, but of course I will, Your Grace!" assured Celine in benevolent triumph. "Never fear, my honey. I will always be ready to guide you! I will always be eager to protect you! I can forever be depended upon to keep my silly fool's career-advancing no matter what nonsense he continues getting himself into!"

As today's Countess de Montfort spoke, over five centuries of illustrious female ancestors (several nude) observed through portraits crafted by artists from El Greco, Velasquez, and Van Dyck to Cezanne, Klimt, and Modigliani. Each earlier famous grand courtesan now registered her deep approval of, signaled her immense pride in, their clan's present leader.

I

To the left, beneath the likenesses of two other *Montfort Ladies*, one painted by Gainsborough, the other by Delacroix, stood a shiny, expertly tuned, concert grand piano with an open top.

At last she wriggling free of Markovsky's needfully-lecherous clutches, Celine first, rising to feet, next, adjusting her cobalt-blue silk opera gown, then, hurried daintily to the instrument.

"Let's have some music!" she announced, her long, heavy, cherry-blond locks tossed back with a single motion of the lovely head. "I am giving my next live concert on Saturday evening, here in Paris at the *Garnier l'Opéra*. Since Your Grace will unfortunately be away at that silly, boring, men's NATO conference in Brussels, he will be unable to attend. But no worry! Your Grace can tonight enjoy a special, intimate, private foretaste of what I later intend to play for the public while he is gone. I hope Your Grace always enjoys my humble effort."

Gifted ladylike fingers commanded the keyboard.

As they sped the eighty-eight white and black hammer tips, the epic notes of Beethoven's Piano Concerto No. 5 in E-Flat Major filled memorable the entire townhouse. Elsewhere in the mansion, lady's maid Frédérique and the other servants instantly set down appointed chores to listen to their mistress's stirring performance. As do all great artists, this one too made the audience believe a long rehearsed, intricately studied, much pored-over work was easy to perform. If it's known to history as the "Emperor Concerto," anyone hearing a rendition by Countess de Montfort would naturally conclude this piece is named the *"Empress."*

"Beautiful, beautiful! As always, you are absolutely superb, my fair darling!" extolled Markovsky with immense appreciation when the concerto was complete. His touch of Celine's unblemished skin was now replaced by a massage of her equally fine music.

The gent's words soon waxed melodramatic:

Celine then played *The Goldberg Variations* by Bach and then Piano Concerto No. 3 in C by Prokofiev.

II

"Bravo! Bravo!" roundly interjected adventurer, Intelligence chief Brigadier Erdal Aslan, he entering the salon abruptly from down the way. The spymaster was dressed today in a khaki military outfit, shined black cavalry boots, a 50 hollow nose bullet-clip semiautomatic belt. In his mid-fifties, with an athletic physique, the Turkish expatriate was strikingly handsome in a rugged, non-pretty boy manner. "Bravo! Bravo! I can't think of the last time I've heard such a brilliant performance! I could have intruded earlier, but I thought it only appropriate first to let my gifted young lady finish several of the famous pieces she's so well mastered."

The pianist halted as Prokofiev's masterpiece neared its climax. "Brigadier Aslan! Brigadier Aslan!"

Celine scrambled out from behind the instrument.

"Brigadier Aslan! Brigadier Aslan!"

She made her beloved old warrior a deep, yearning curtsey.

"Bless you, Brigadier Aslan! I'm so happy you enjoy hearing me play the piano!"

"I love nothing better in all the world than hearing you play, Mme. Celine. I just wish my busy, hectic schedule permitted me far more time to come and listen!"

"Be confident," the general added, "I own all my young lady's CDs. Whenever I feel down, whenever I feel anxious, indecisive, I turn on one of these recordings. Nothing I hear is lovelier, more inspiring than listening to my young lady play her piano! Where would I ever be without my young lady's music to keep me on a steady, firm, confident course!"

"Bless you, my dearest Brigadier Aslan!"

As on every occasion since this duo first met at the younger of the pair's sixth birthday party when Aslan was recruited as a last-minute replacement for a clown previously engaged, now-adult Celine instantly snapped to attention. She delivered her commander as steadfast, devoted, and enthusiastic a salute as when the buddies were originally introduced.

Brigadier Aslan!"

After he first motioned to inspect his aide-de-camp's uniform, next signalled everything was as usual in perfect order, the old warrior then smiled his warm, hearty approval. Finally, he bowed to Celine respectfully and clicked the heels of his shined black cavalry boots.

"So, all is in proper order, Brigadier Aslan? So, I am still your *Good Little Soldier?*"

"No need fear, Mme. Celine. You are forever my *Good Little Soldier.*"

"Bless you, Brigadier Aslan! I'm always ready and eager to serve! Night and Day! Storm and sunshine! Winter and Summer! Advance and in retreat! From here to China and back! Even on the dark side of the Moon! Just give me the assignment, and I'm immediately off to perform it! I promise to accomplish any task you give me I'll do it boldly, decisively, successfully, at once! I won't waste a second! I'll 'take the high ground!' I'll capture the enemy hill or fortress! I'll seize the far shore of the river! I'll secure the foreign beachhead! I'll master the critical salient! I'll lift the longest, most brutal siege!"

"For me, Brigadier Aslan," she promised, "no bridge will ever, ever be a bridge too far!"

The girl, at last, fell silent.

She bent over, hands resting on her knees, out of breath, heart racing.

Her thick cherry blond hair reached the waxed, hardwood panel floor.

"So I know, Mme. Celine!" promised Brigadier Aslan. "You are my most tireless, most dedicated, most gifted lieutenant!" The general's powerful arms could untwist horseshoes and, as his devoted young friend often requested, promptly twist the iron pieces back into their original shape.

If today, she was dressed in a long strapless gown, pantyhose, and heels, Celine mysteriously sensed herself once again clothed in a sixth birthday party's new pinafore, once again she wearing bobbysocks and flat mary-janes. If the present chatelaine's thick cherry blond hair fell freely below her bare shoulders, she felt it tied in little girl pigtails and bright ribbons.

The old warrior glanced at his *Rolex* watch.

"If you want a new assignment to 'boldly perform' Mme. Celine, my Sweetheart, go and fetch President Markovsky. It's time for him to depart for the NATO conference in Brussels.'"

"At once, Brigadier Aslan!" replied his faithful lieutenant, she once more delivering her commander a deep curtsey and firm, devoted salute.

After adjusting her imaginary pinafore and pigtails, the birthday girl sped off to fulfill her appointed task.

"Now get up at once, Your Grace!" cried the *Good Little Soldier* to President Markovsky, he still busy feeling sorry for himself slouched in an armchair under a portrait of a Montfort Lady painted by Matisse. "Now get up at once, Your Grace! It's time for your to fly to meet the other heads-of-state in Brussels!"

Celine looked back furtively to see if Brigadier Aslan was watching his young aide's performance.

And so he was!

The watchful general returned his faithful junior trooper a fond adult smile and encouraging paternal wink of his eye.

Finally, Aslan raised his two upturned grownup thumbs announcing an experienced superior officer's warm approval.

Markovsky shuffled to his feet.

"Stand still! Don't move! Let me fix you up! Let me be sure you look tip-top! Let me be sure you look *presidential!*" lectured the *Good Little Soldier,* she now serving as drill sergeant to a less than the first-class recruit. "Remember, Your Grace, there's a very important, most crucial diplomatic get-together in Brussels this weekend! Remember, foreigners often judge an entire nation simply by the appearance, by the words given to the press, by the conduct before the television, of that nation's chief executive! Think of the international figure cut for France by General de Gaulle or M. Macron! Think of how Germany is so often visualized in Willy Brandt or Mrs. Merkel! Britain, by Mrs. Thatcher or Tony Blair!"

"For both the good and the bad," instructed the *Good Little Soldier*, "for both the ideal and the not so *ideal*, these men and ladies largely create through their public persona the lasting image the rest of the world possesses of that particular leader's entire country and all his or her countrymen–and *countrywomen*. Remember, Your Grace is not simply going to Brussels himself but is also going as the most visible, the most distinctive representative of all his 67 million fellow citizens!"

"Yes," answered Markovsky, compliant. "And don't you ever forget it, Your Grace!" "No, I will not. I promise." "Good!"

As she fiddled with Markovsky's jacked, reoriented his tie, *The Good Little Soldier* hummed La Marseillaise.

"*There*," she declared at last. "Your Grace now looks splendid! Your Grace looks ready to take on the world!"

"Don't you think so, too, Brigadier Aslan?" questioned his devoted young aide.

"Indeed me. Celine, my gifted, faithful *Sweetheart!*" The old warrior now turned to a subordinate. "First Sergeant Lefebvre—"

"Yes, Sir!" promptly answered the NCO, stamping his right boot as he delivered his commander a firm, loyal salute. A veteran of more than a dozen heroic campaigns, the NCO's strong, wide chest was covered with much-deserved ribbons of distinction and well-earned medals for valor.

"First Sergeant Lefebvre, take President Markovsky to the limousine. It's time he departed for the NATO conference in Brussels."

"Yes, Sir!" instantly replied the be-ribboned, be-medaled NCO, again stamping right boot and delivering his commander a firm, loyal salute.

Markovsky was unceremoniously hustled to his vehicle.

Trundle, trundle, trundle, receding trundle.

"So, I've set the President off at last!" sighed Celine when she and Brigadier Aslan were once more alone. "I guess no matter what station a girl manages to achieve in life, she still ultimately discovers–*A woman's work is never done.*"

"Bah! Nonsense! That's much too pessimistic a way of looking at the world, my influential, kingmaker, path-breaking Dear," injected France's adventurous Intelligence chief, he stroking Celine's thick, cherry blonde locks affectionately. "A common, tawdry, unappreciated existence might be the fate of most females but certainly not for you! Certainly not for you, my *Good Little Soldier!*"

"You, Sweetheart, in contrast," pledged her hero, "are set for a grand, special kind of destiny! I am sure the historians of the future will prove your Brigadier is absolutely correct!"

"Perhaps," replied Celine, not totally convinced. "Only time will tell."

Just to the left, beneath a picture of a Montfort Lady painted by Renoir and atop a waist-high mahogany *Chippendale* chest-of-drawers with shined brass shelf-handles and lace coverlet, stood a framed color photograph of then eleven-year-old Rolande de Montfort. She, clad in a frilly, white, first communion dress. A large blue silk bow crowned the child's even then abundant fiery red hair. Beside the picture, it delicately folded and placed back in the turquoise color envelope, sat her letter: *"Dearest Mama, your Missy needs to go away for a while–"*

Rather than dashed-off on cheap scratch paper in an illegible scrawl, the letters' words were set down on a piece of the family's custom-ordered stationary; the recorded sentences in an elegant feminine script. No evidence could be detected of the rapid speed and fierce determination generating this cryptic message.

Recently returned from sending Rolande off on her unique mission, Brigadier Aslan brought the letter to the girl's parent, unopened. "Gentleman," the warrior insisted, "don't read ladies' mail."

"And never forget my *Good Little Soldier's* globetrotting younger daughter!" encouraged the spymaster, still stroking the mother's cheery blond locks affectionately. "Rolande, too, is clearly set on an unusual, special, historic destiny!"

Celine smiled, tender, wistful.

Pensive, maternal eyes were catching sight of a cherished offspring were now located far beyond the room.

"So, Brigadier Aslan, our *Missy* does possess a *calling*?" "Yes, Mme. Celine. Our girl indeed possesses a *calling*."

"So, our Treasure is summoned to fulfill a glorious task?"

"Without doubt, Sweetheart."

Rolande's mother pondered.

"Is our *Missy* being successful at her undertaking?"

"But of course she will succeed, Mme. Celine" guaranteed Brigadier Aslan. "How could the child ever possibly fail when one considers the remarkable Mama from whose womb she came!"

THE ʟADIES GARDEN TRUST

LIBERATION IS AT HAND!–PROCLAIMED PARISIAN newspapers of every political stripe following autumn's belated entrance into the weary, summer-ravaged city.

Victory has come! –shouted the press at its most fulsome.

The long and shameful occupation is finally driven out!

The enemy is expelled!

We are finally free!

Few other moments in our nation's entire illustrious history– pledged one editorial**–can compare to this triumphant, joyous occasion!**

Let us all join hands and sing in one common voice of celebration! urged another editorial**–Yes, all of us! Those on the Right, on the Left and everyone in between! Today is no time to waste on divisive politics. Let us all unite and give thanks to something more significant and more lasting than our mortal, false selves!**

If such purple prose is typically reserved for celebrating a great military success, for memorializing a national hero, or announcing an historic sports triumph, few men and women picking up their favorite newspaper at street corner kiosk or outside family front door, believed this current hyperbole inappropriate. At any event, who could blame the scribblers for letting their emotions get slightly out of hand? After all the residents of the French capital recently suffered through, a bit of mild-boasting, harmless-embellishment was only fitting!

Cathedral bells soon rang out, as well.

Artillery firing added salutes.

Vehicles honked symphonically.

Tugboats hooted joyfully.

Not to be left out, crowds roared and stomped their feet in rhythm.

At expressed presidential order, massive, colorful fireworks displayed was arranged to illuminate the Paris sky that evening for over an hour.

As far as the two and-a-half-million inhabitants of the city proper and the eleven million-odd residents of the greater Ile de France metropolitan area were concerned, the summer just passed felt as if they had each barely survived a long and difficult siege. Even today, veterans of that crisis uniformly insist those dismal months were close akin to being subjected to brutal martial law.

From early May through mid-October, not a drop of rain fell; there blew hardly a single refreshing breeze. Thermometers never dipped under one hundred degrees, even at soupy night. Record-breaking, almanac-capturing, dog-day weather engulfed each nook and cranny of the city and her extensive suburbs; invaded each aspect, element of her citizens' personal lives. Sections of significant highways buckled. With no rain and hardly one sustained gust of wind for months-on-end to disburse it, dense, sickly-yellow, foul-smelling, eye-irritating smog forced the closure of all airports. Sewage lines and water mains burst, creating all the expected unhygienic consequences.

Individuals caught outside in this hazy, unhealthy furnace, oppressive temperature, sweltering humidity, exhausted all voluntary physical movement or firm mental calculation after only a few minutes. Industrial production plummeted. Famous museums and historical sites were otherwise jammed with crowds, often closed by noon for lack of public interest. Some illustrious homes or celebrated galleries never even opened at all. For an extended period, the usually crammed *Metro* was near empty.

The regional power grid proved inadequate to service the sudden rush of electricity demanded by millions of customers for air conditioners and ceiling fans. At least twice a month, the utility system broke down and *The City of Light* was embraced for long hours by burning, sweaty, near-suffocating darkness. Ambulances daily wailed mournful sirens as victims of either sun-stroke or heat exhaustion were sped to already-congested hospital emergency rooms. Scores of persons, either aged or in fragile health, did not survive—establishing a gruesome, dubious record. Even some four-legged members of the population fell victim.

Usually, Parisians compelled to venture outdoors under similar conditions were guaranteed a measure of relief under the cool, deep, sheltering, maternal woods of an enclosed garden running parallel to the Right embankment. Not this time, unfortunately. Drought, early on forced the ancient oak, plane, and chestnut trees to prematurely abandon their heavy, comforting green mantels. By no later than mid-June, their great, wide branches withered and bare, the trees appeared to human viewers as pained, sorrowful as in coldest, dark by 5 PM, winter.

Without the protective shade tree canopies typically provided, water sprayed upon grass evaporated almost as soon as it was rinsed. Bright green lawns of late April were scorched, dark brown no later than the second week of June. Lovingly kept expansive beds of wisteria, clematis, roses, anemones, hydrangeas, crocus, snapdragons, tulips, begonias, delphiniums, and hollyhocks withered away despite the greatest, most tender feminine human care. Duck, fish, rowing and children's toy boat-sailing ponds dried up.

Drinking fountains were useless. The instruments' bronze or copper handles became so fiery hot that people desperate to quench their thirst soon found the nozzles too painful to touch for even one brave moment. As to the alternative of a tasty *Italian Ice* available at nearby stalls, these treats melted in hand before the eager purchasers, both young and elderly, could manage taking more than two or three yummy, yearning licks. As a result, it left anxious fingers sticky with nowhere to clean them and sorrowful throats just as agonizingly parched as before.

The water level of the dark, murky Seine dropped a historic number of meters. In doing so, this unprecedented dip revealed some fascinating discoveries about daily life during Gallic, Roman, and Merovingian times. Several additional months needed to pass, however, before the weather was cool enough and the air sufficiently dry to inspire archeologists like Pascale Kedari's polymath stepfather Richard Castellane to venture out of their air-conditioned offices or lecture halls to investigate and catalog these amazing new sites.

Elsewhere, blistering, heat-absorbing cobblestone and asphalt quickly burned feet through shoes and even army boots. Flower bouquets and decorative plants sold in florist shops died nearly as soon as they were removed from refrigerators. Stakes and obstacle course races at Longchamps were canceled lest the valuable thoroughbred horses become ill galloping or jumping under the oppressive sun. Petty urban crime dropped precipitously as purse-snatching, shop-lifting, and vandalism required far too much physical and mental strain to commit in the current heat.

Grand avenues, long boulevards, and wide public plazas notorious for the 24-hour roar and incessant vehicle congestion were now often silent, deserted. Historically reliable outbreaks of street protest and soapbox-pontificating failed to materialize beneath the baking sun and sickly-yellow air pollution. Even diversions like sex, eavesdropping, gossip, and being a peeping-tom proved too exhaustive undertakings for their many veteran practitioners. Not once on record did Paris experience such a long, miserable, torpid ordeal.

Then, seemingly miraculous, just as the debilitated population came to fear those sweaty, smothering, dog-days might last forever, they were gone. The hideous siege abruptly lifted. The brutal enemy withdrew of its own accord. No wonder then that all those normally cynical, worldly-wise members of the press cried-out the glorious news like happy, innocent children.

Snap, snap, snap, snap, snap–of complicated Japanese camera

Gadget rewound

Snap, snap, snap, snap, snap.

"Goodness, gracious me!" exclaimed the melodic voice of skillful amateur photographer Countess Marie-Therese-Celine de Montfort. If she a kingmaker long acknowledged too, as Europe's most skillful pianist, this lady did not achieve such lofty fame through becoming a mere one-trick-pony.

This morning, the Countess wore: a large white chapeau; a string of natural pearls, a short chartreuse sleeveless dress, sheerest pantyhose, and a new pair of red spiked-high heels. The grand dame's fetching, the insightful face was deeply agitated as a camera in sculpted hands, she inspected her favorite semi-enclosed public garden early that same blessedly cool Tuesday morning in late October.

Snap, snap, snap, snap, snap.

It once a riot of vibrant, beckoning: red, blue, green, pink, white, yellow, orange, lavender, purple, the garden was now only a mass of dead, dusty army brown, Stalin gray, and funereal black.

"Goodness, gracious me! As the Virgin is my witness, I declare I have never seen anything as disastrous as this! And hopefully, I'll never need to see it again! Goodness, gracious! How's a witless female like me ever going to summon the wherewithal to fix this catastrophe! Well, I will try my feeble best! First, I've got to take some more photos—a lot more photos!"

Snap, snap, snap, snap, snap.

Click, click

"Oh, botheration!" declared fragrant Celine. "Oh, botheration! It's run-out!'

Soon adding confidently: "No real trouble, it will just take me a moment."

Removing the finished roll of film, dropping it into her white *Hermes Birkin* handbag, she promptly reloaded the camera with a fresh roll.

"There! Now back to work!

Snap. Snap, snap, snap, snap.

"Maybe one day," talented photographer Celine mused, "I might even get hired for doing this!"

Snap, snap, snap, snap, snap of the camera

Like her younger daughter Rolande, now embarked on a cross-country self-discovery romp, Mama too escaped the capital's dreadful summer. In parent's case, she retreating in mid-April to the *Montfort Ladies'* domed, Ionic-colonnaded, Neoclassical manor amidst the stunning French Alps. It was a property first owned by Madame de Pompadour, then Madame de Stael, still later by Sarah Bernhardt. This queenly residence did more than provide its present chatelaine with thought-provoking views of pristine forests, snow-capped mountain crags, thundering waterfalls, many a plunging abyss, and mammoth blue glacier.

Located at over seven thousand feet above sea level, it caressed by a smooth, cloudless, aquamarine sky, daytime temperature at this Alpine hideaway even in the most torpid days of August never exceeded fifty-five degrees. Nights often turned bitter cold, and well-stocked red, yellow, and blue flames danced a merry jig in fireplaces throughout the mansion. Upstairs, in a vast, four-poster, canopied *Queen Anne* oak bed, Celine curled up into a ball beneath several thick blankets, wearing wool socks to warm her feet.

Snap, snap, snap, further camera snaps.

Whenever she "mountaineering," Celine was sure always to wear a coat or sports jacket, pullover sweater, long scarf, a thick woolen skirt, new tights, and "sensible shoes." At these lofty heights, her headgear possessed a long white or red ribbon tied around her slender neck. So, as to prevent a gust of wind suddenly carrying her huge, vulnerable chapeau off into the incalculable, romantic, *Medieval Saga* distance.

Each day, while situated high above the clouds, the air fresh and cool, she sitting dainty in a comfortable antique red damask armchair, her meals prepared by a personal chef served on *Sevres* porcelain atop a *Louis XV-Style* oak table with hand-sewn silk Pre-1789 cover, Celine grew pensive. She spent nostalgic hours contemplating the virginal alpine landscape. This magnificent panorama stretching out to the horizon as if created by God specifically for one tender lady's enjoyment could not make the viewer reflective.

As the unquestioned monarch of this miniature, picturesque domain, Celine on a number of occasions considered ordering her offspring to come and attend court. She, calling them hither so their Mama might press the darlings to her welcoming maternal bust for the remainder of the three's collective *born-in-the-wrong-century* lives. Here, at Chateau Montfort, halfway up eternally snow-capped Mt. St. Anne, Mama could be certain "my best genes and *DNA*" were forever shielded from all the world's vain ugliness, grasping materialism, unfaithful promise. Here, at secluded alpine Chateau Montfort, the Countess might keep her "two precious creations" invulnerable to evil, pain and disillusionment.

Snap, snap, snap, snap.

Twice, Mama went so far as reaching for an ornate telephone with a secured line to issue her instructions—she even turning the first four of seven relevant numbers on an old fashion rotary dial before regretfully halting. As much as biological instinct urged her to proceed intellectually, Celine knew it was in her daughters' ultimate best interest for their possessive Mama to set the telephone aside.

"Don't worry," their parent concluded, "my *Two Little Things* will manage on their own– After all, I created them!"

Rolande and her half-sister Ferdinande de Godefroy were, like the two girls' common parent—*Montfort Ladies.* From the Renaissance onward, in every succeeding generation unbroken since before Diane of Poitiers, the clan's daughters become grand courtesans. Each girl freely assumes and no less admirably fulfills her obligation to shape daintily, command modestly, direct ever-so demure, the entire political, diplomatic, cultural, and religious life of Europe.

"And" observed Celine, rewinding her camera today in the drought-ravaged garden, "we do it all without we ever even once wearing trousers!"

Last week, upon receiving urgent pleas from the capital to provide her much-needed presence, Celine, at last, shut up her manor above the clouds and returned by helicopter and a private jet to Paris. Both flying machines. She operated personally.

Snap, snap, snap, additional energetic camera snap.

Circumnavigating the Continental Style **Pascale Kedari Memorial Garden** for an hour—first, traveling north to south—then, east to west—around a second, third time—Celine took four long rolls of color photographs. All the over two hundred images she took and later developed at home might easily be the work of a distinguished professional. "Who knows," the amateur remarked with just pride, "perhaps I missed my true calling!"

"Ah, yes!" soon declared Celine. "I must not forget taking an image of this dear old chestnut tree over *there*."

Snap, snap, snap, snap.

"Next, I must record this poor flower bed I worked on so much by myself last year, down *here*."

Snap, snap, snap, fervent camera snap.

"Ooh! Ooh! Look! Look!!" now exclaimed some of Countess de Montfort's legion of fans, they entering the garden from the opposite direction. "Look! Look! It's our Celine! It's Our Celine!"

The newcomers waved to their idol in exciting admiration.

Next, this crowd of all ages scrambled down the gravel path to get a better look at this so marvelous and unexpected sight.

Each fan took out her camera to obtain a priceless image of the grand lady.

Photo, photo, photo, photo, fans' desperately loyal photo

"We love you, Our Celine!"

"We love you, Our Celine!"

"Now and forever!"

As always, the Countess responded graciously to her avid disciples. She offering them all, she presenting each: first, a deep, deep curtsey; next, a demure aristocratic smile; finally, a humble dip of head.

Photo, photo, photo, photo, devotees' passionately committed photo

"Bless you, bless you, Our Celine!" cried her apostles with lifelong gratitude.

Their heroine instantly rewarded each of her followers with yet a second deep curtsey, yet a second demure aristocratic smile, still another dip of the titled head.

"Bless you, Our Celine!" replied her overjoyed admirers. "Bless you. Our Celine!"

The Countess then signed many autographs. Each note was personalized and written in Madame's elegant, distinctive feminine script.

To: Marie-Claude from her special friend Celine

To: Bernadette from her longtime buddy Celine

For: Marie-Helene with best wishes from her devoted pal Celine

For: Rosalie, hoping all the best, her good friend always, Celine.

To: Louise, in memory of our wonderful meeting, your own Celine.

"Being so famous, being so admired is a tremendous honor," mused the Countess, silently. "It moves me, touches me immensely. However, with such wide prestige also comes grave responsibility. I must be sure to conduct myself in a fashion demonstrating I continue remaining worthy of my followers' love and appreciation. What does Shakespeare say? *Uneasy rests the head that wears the crown.*"

I

Madame de Montfort intended to distribute her photographs at an emergency luncheon she called for noon tomorrow at cream color, palatial No. 3 Rue Artemis. As chairman of *The Ladies Garden Trust*–she positively loathed *chairperson*–the Countess believed it both her duty and obligation since returning to Paris to daily inspect and evaluate how the recent drought and long heat plague affected the historic greenery. These unique woods, celebrated flowerbeds and thoughtfully-winding tree-sheltered gravel paths also served as the inspiration for a number of *Impressionist* masterpieces.

Three of these priceless paintings Countess de Montfort obtained herself! One canvas was the work of Cezanne, the second was crafted by Renoir, the third by Pissarro. No need she is taking out insurance. If stolen, no sum of dirty cash would ever make up for this great art's loss! Besides, no need to worry. Paintings of the famous are instantly recognizable to hundreds of millions around the world. It could never be fenced. The thieves would quickly discover that their loot was more a burden in their grubby hands than a grand prize!

Countess de Montfort understood that nearly all the other members of the *Ladies Garden Trust* board of supervisors deeply respected their longtime chairman's eight-straight-European cups and eight-national-prize-contests-in-succession-expertise at gardening. Mme. Toledano, Mme. Lamanceau, Baroness de Clignancourt, and the other gracious dames would never challenge their leader's impeccable wisdom concerning all matters floral. Each lady could be relied upon to support her chairman's decision that this year's record-setting drought and heatwave made necessary a no less unprecedented expenditure to restore this paradigm of metropolitan greenery to its original, poetic, *Impressionist* beauty.

Since these repairs (beginning next spring) would coincide with the enactment of President Markovsky's bitterly-divisive new domestic policy, however, Countess de Montfort was insistent her exquisite woods and flowerbeds should not fall victim to "the men's filthy politics." In a time of high unemployment and general economic recession, "soapbox-demagogues" and "whining leftists" might readily select "trivial maintenance" to aristocratic neighborhoods as an excellent rabble-rousing, as a reliable vote-pandering target.

"The best way of avoiding the men's electioneering hubbub," Countess de Montfort told the board, was for the ladies to endorse their chairman's "trivial maintenance" project without descent. By winning unanimous support from a board whose husbands or gentleman chums represented all of France's respectable political parties, she argued, the park could "escape becoming collateral damage to the men's stupid office-seeking."

The chairman requested a unanimous endorsement.

Not the usual 9-1 vote of approval she normally received.

Instead, 10-0.

No dissent

Unanimous!

Considering the chairman's tumultuous relationship with the final, so often hold-out member of the board, however, unanimity was not at all a foregone conclusion.

If Countess de Montfort wields vast indirect power, exerts tremendous unobserved influence over western society, it's because she understands *what men want*. Persuading presidents, kings, prime ministers, plutocrats, or strongmen with dark glasses into seeing matters this lady's way has never been a problem. Currently, though, Madame confronted a far more daunting opponent—another woman.

"GIRLS AREN'T GOOD AT MATH"

LADIES GARDEN TRUST BOARD MEMBERS Countess Marie-Therese-Celine de Montfort and Mrs. Robertson Mackenzie Villers took a strong dislike to one another from almost the instant the pair first crossed paths. Neither was really to blame for what followed nor could be accused of intentionally permitting the quarrel to fester. Neither woman failed over time to volunteer amicable solutions or rejected outright any serious peace proposal suggested by her opponent. Still, the conflict dragged on.

Countess de Montfort and Mrs. Villers each sincerely judged herself to be the injured party. And according to both the grand courtesan's and the academic researcher's separate interpretations of life, both were also each correct. Two such highly intelligent, gifted, and seeming hopelessly-incompatible individuals were likely never to see anything eye-to-eye. Let alone, they one day become devoted, genteel, lady-exiting-a-car-properly–feminine chums.

As on all previous occasions, this scrappy duo's latest disagreement was, in fact, peripheral to the real issue dividing them. Mrs. Villers was as fiercely committed to preserving the city's most beautiful, picturesque, enclosed garden as was the Countess. She merely advocated employing different tactics. The true source of the two's long, bitter, mutual animosity was both more complicated and simple.

In the candid appraisal of no less physically-attractive Ashraf Kermanshani (Parisians were unaware her marriage to late-husband had been only a common-law arrangement), *Messalina,* as the Iranian-American derisively referred to Celine, was the living manifestation of all the false, conniving, mercenary social values her rival fled back in the United States. From the outset, she never considered Messalina the remarkable, trailblazing heroine countless millions of adoring Europeans proclaimed. Quite the opposite! In Ashraf's judgment, Messalina was remarkable," "trailblazing," only in that she was the first to successfully amalgamate two traditional and highly negative female stereotypes.

One: the arrogant, hedonistic, *well-let-then-eat-cake* Marie-Antoinette figure–she convinced the entire universe exists solely for obeying its queen's every passing, harebrained, narcissist whim.

Two: the parasitic, scheming, sexual-predator Herodias–all her worldly attainments, including John the Baptist's head on a silver platter, achieved through making powerful but weak-willed males emotionally-dependent on the pleasure a certain woman provides them in bed.

That, following over five decades of hard-won legal and social progress, Messalina remained to tens of millions of her sex the object of undying, unquestioning, self-demeaning, pagan cult-worship– was, in Ashraf's opinion, not just distasteful but troubling. If, rather than being regarded as equals to men, European women wished instead only to be misogynist stereotypes, Messalina, her opponent feared, might be a far more accurate projection of *what women want* than is desirable to think.

"Yes, Messalina is very charming, smart, and pretty," Ashraf conceded. "Yes, she's a countess related to Charlemagne and Otto the Great. Yes, Messalina owns portraits of her ancestors painted by Memling, Botticelli, Durer, and Titian. Yes, she's undoubtedly today's most brilliant classical pianist. One, who also gets appointed to chair every last charity fund-raising drive or good-works committee. But in the end, like the notorious Roman empress before her, this Messalina too is still just a whore! And whatever degree of real influence that particular *working-girl* exercises over European society will last only so long as she's got distinguished *johns* to service!"

"Ultimately," summarized Ashraf, "you can't rise horizontal!"

Countess de Montfort's view of her rival was no less decided. "Mrs. Villers needs to get pregnant! If that *Smartypants* American *Know-it-All* doesn't start making babies soon, she'll become insufferable!

She'll turn into one of those frustrated, self-loathing, frigid, *Angry Women* who cut their hair short and wear trousers."

"Meddling with nature" further warns the celebrated pianist, "and don't forget it is–*mother* nature–trying to stop things God always meant to be–inevitably leads to bad consequences! For example, without motherhood enabling its full development, the unrivaled affectionate and nurturing, unequaled soft and gentle aspect of the female character is permanently stunted. Without experiencing motherhood, a woman who, according to nature, should be warm, loving, protective, becomes instead, a *Mrs. Villers*."

Blessed with: a lovely face and excellent figure, great legs, fine bust; a charming, endearing personality (when she was choosing to make it so); already possessed of several wealthy aristocratic suitors needing a consort—"Mrs. Villers should have no trouble getting married, becoming regnant, and then she and her ensuing brood being more than well provided for!" The present "morose disagreeable, *Ms. Radical Feminist*" could soon be transformed into a happy, congenial, *Stay-at-home-Mom* eagerly knitting sweaters, scarfs, and booties. "She, often recounting her darling Marie-Jeanne, Marie-Chantal, and Marie-Madeleine's first words and steps, she gleefully bombarding her guests with endless baby pictures."

Socially and politically influential Countess de Montfort could swift negotiate the marriage, too! She quickly settles all the arrangements! "But likely, *Liberated* Mrs. Villers would be offended."

I

Born in Tabriz, Iran but living since age six in Amherst, Massachusetts, USA, her parents devoting almost every waking moment to their famous older daughter Golbihar's world-renowned figure skating career, Ashraf Kermanshani might have easily developed into "one of those frustrated, self-loathing, frigid, *Angry Women* who cut their hair short and wear trousers." However, she didn't. Nor did she become, as Celine long assumed, a *Ms. Radical Feminist.* Instead, this "S*martypants American*" found her true interests elsewhere.

If her relatives claimed that Ashraf's celebrated attribute first manifested itself soon after she arrived in America when she was observed cataloging her dolls, it, in fact, emerged still earlier—back in Tabriz, when she started counting her toes. The child's remarkable gift for higher mathematics, long overlooked by her parents, was denied the sufficient level of early enhanced special tutoring required to achieve complete blossoming. That her ability developed to the great extent it did, all the same, is a painful testament to how much even additional God-given talent was permitted to simply wither unappreciated on the vine.

Entering at age just fourteen and graduating in only three years with a perfect 4.0-grade average, first in her class, *Phi Beta Kappa, Summa Cum Laude,* acquiring a degree in Advanced Mathematics, a minor in Nineteenth-Century Literature, Ashraf established the highest academic record in her prestigious women's college's long history. Next, she set out to obtain a *Doctorate.*

In graduate school, the girl applied to her own intellectual pursuits the same unmatched beauty and faultless grace exhibited by her older sister Golbihar on the Olympic skating rink. Teenage Ashraf authored a steady series of increasingly more brilliant and innovative academic papers. Each one in succession either disproved a hitherto judged eternal, sacrosanct principle of her complicated subject or introduced to the field yet another groundbreaking, original concept–*The Kermanshani Equation, Kermanshani's Critique, Kermanshani's Razor.*

"Solving number problems, devising new number theories is such awesome fun!" she giggled. "I can't imagine anything more exciting!"

Soon, Ashraf's professors, all-male, permitted the remarkable child to forgo class attendance and graduate seminars so that she might not be distracted speedily advancing as far as possible on an independent, perhaps even historic, path of mathematical theory.

Besides, none of the gents could keep up with their students, anyway.

If ancient perceived-wisdom declares: *Girls aren't good at Math,* one pretty adolescent in short skirt and heels was so skilled, so gifted at the subject, that she even devised mathematical loops, jumps and spins all the Dear's very own. Like a great Olympic figure skater, young Miss Kermanshani, the result to countless hours-upon-countless hours of unbroken study, repeated memorization, tedious preparation, appear to the eyes of captivated audiences as spontaneous, carefree play.

When Miss Kermanshani executed all those delicate, complicated moves, they looked so easy, appeared so relaxed and simple. Given her innocent, vulnerable, ladylike character, perfect beauty, unblemished race from this cerebral athlete was only to be expected.

The entire middle-aged, masculine, tenured faculty was deeply impressed, immensely taken with the gifted youngster. Each instructor soon regarded Ashraf as *his* own exceptional performing monkey, as *his* own faithful prodigy, as *his* own loyal mascot.

"No better proof exists," these gents declared, "that brains and looks aren't mutually exclusive!" Each strenuously claimed that *he* originally discovered Ashraf, that *he* was the one counseling her first, that *he* alone set *his* remarkable child on the path to academic glory.

"*My* Ashraf is someone truly special!"–gushed every paunchy, balding, male professor on more than few occasions. "*My* little protegée is bound for history!" "*My* Sweetheart is a paramount mind not to be seen again!" Just being able to point-out that "he excused the brainy girl from taking *his* course," bubbled instructors, was well-worth mentioning in *his* lecture, including in *his* grant application, business query, press interview, or *his* professional autobiography!

The university administration was sure to both mention and photograph its diligent, obedient Persian cat in all student recruiting pamphlets, in all fund-raising pleas to wealthy alumni. "Pretty number machine"-Ashraf was evoked in every request to the state capital and Washington DC for additional government financial aid! She even once appeared on a *PBS* television documentary about young immigrant scientists.

"Given the Sweetheart's strict, conservative upbringing, one, leaving her unspoiled by that *Women's Lib* mumbo-jumbo," she could be depended upon never to act up or talk back. She would always do precisely what men instructed, never try dope, say anything controversial, or embarrass her mentors through entanglement in sexual scandal. "Likely," reflected the self-satisfied male faculty, "our gifted little virgin hasn't yet even once held a boy's hand!"

If still to finish her *Doctorate*, Ashraf was nonetheless often invited to speak at major learned conferences. While still to complete her graduate school requirements, Ashraf was often allowed to publish articles in the most distinguished, highly-regarded quarterlies. Any time an international dignitary, political big-shot, business tycoon, or wealthy alumnus visited the university, members of the administration instantly trotted out their star student to greet the power-broker, philanthropist, or celebrity.

"It's all so-so very awesome!" Miss Kermanshani would remark obediently, she curtseying deep, her timid brown eyes cast to the floor. "It's all so-so much more awesome than any girl like me could ever imagine!" She was then dutifully adding: "It could never possibly have happened without all the guidance and encouragement of my brilliant professors and the help of this so-so awesome university."

Upon requesting a part-time job to acquire needed extra spending money away from home, Miss Kermanshani was asked to direct some undergraduate courses. She proved to be both a natural and very able instructor. Rather than stirring jealousy among other students near her own age, the young scholar's friendly, eager, elucidating teaching method won her instead, the pupils' great admiration. She made the most complex mathematical problems and scientific formulas instantly look so simple, pretty, compelling. Above all: "so much fun!"

If Ashraf never *graded on the curve* or granted additional days to finish take-home exams, her firm but reassuring, challenging but empathetic teaching style raised the grades of every single student in her classes. Including those of the people forever sitting in the back row and never raising their hand. Each person felt that Ashraf was his or her own personal devoted tutor. One who held a special concern in seeing that particular individual succeed as far as possible. Word of Miss Kermanshani's unique skill swift spread throughout the campus. It was not long before dozens of people from other departments, with no great interest in this girl's subject, asked to audit. All those privileged with the chance to hear this *Brainy Arab Kid* lecture, roundly agreed that when she explained Higher Mathematics, this usually quite intimidating field became: *"terribly awesome."*

"She's amazing!

"Marvelous!"

Inspiring!"

"This girl is a once in a century phenomenon!" proclaimed all her listeners. "She makes it all so easy to understand and deeply appreciate!"

It appeared there lay before Miss Kermanshani, a splendid academic career.

When she was informing her older sister Golbihar, the world-famous, multiple-Olympic gold medalist figure skater about being offered a teaching position at her former undergrad women's college, Golbihar—no stranger to tedious, repetitive, lengthy practice, dull, extended concentration, to *applying herself*–wisely counseled against a hasty decision.

"It won't be long, Ashraf," she assured the younger of gifted pair, "before you receive similar offers from places still more prestigious! From institutions providing far higher salaries and generous professional rewards!"

Wearing a short, pink, ladies figure skating outfit, Golbihar demonstrated joy at her little sister's success by promptly executing three perfect quadruple twirls far above the rink. "You're one of the best mathematicians there is! Or ever will be! You're a champion in more than only the *Olympics*! Just wait for a little longer, Love, and you can choose between at least a dozen teaching jobs! Tenure-track! Both here, in America and Europe!"

"And when you at last make a decision," promised Golbihar, immediately executing yet a fourth perfect quadruple twirl *Kermanshani Move* far above the rink, "I'll come to the school and deliver a special figure skating exhibition in your honor!"

Then, only a week later, Ashraf's academic adviser Dr. James Hardwick, chairman of the university's Advanced Mathematics

Department, provided his protegée the ultimate, grandest compliment of all. So unprecedented, so nimble, so delicate, impressive, were his star pupil's newest set of dainty intellectual loops, spins, twirls and jumps, that her professor decided taking credit for them, himself.

What followed didn't end well, at least not for the young doctoral candidate. All that effusive middle-aged masculine praise and admiration, she discovered, came at a price—one, it was now time for Ashraf to pay.

"This is simply how things operate in the larger, bigger, grown-up world, Dear" explained Dr. Hardwick ominously, after first closing his office door behind. "But don't worry, Honey, you will get your turn too, later. I promise! Have I ever even once lied to you, Darling? Of course not! Neither in the past, not now, nor will I ever speak falsely to you in the future! After all, you are my favorite Persian Pussycat. This is just how it is done in the larger, wider, adult world into which Cutie hopes to be admitted. How the hell do you think someone gets elected Pope? Certainly not by the intervention of the Holy Ghost! How do you think David became king? How do you think Sam Rayburn was chosen to be Speaker? Where would LBJ have ever gotten without he first helping-out Richard Russell?"

"Do this one favor for me today, Sweetheart" said Professor Hardwick, "and you've demonstrated you're now *One of Us*–a loyal comrade–a faithful member of the team. I had to do this too back when you wore diapers–or, I guess by your generation, it was *pampers*. Do this for me today, and my Little Girl is absolutely assured a place at the Big Boys' Table later on. I promise! I guarantee it! What, was it that *Mister Sam* used to say?– 'To get along, go along.'"

As a hint of the still far greater benefits waiting her in the future if she simply agreed to cooperate today, Ashraf was offered: a tenure-track position at the university; a rent-free apartment with balcony bordering an historic, private verdant park; even, weekend use of Dr. Hardwick's *Ferrari*. All this, could be hers beginning tomorrow morning, if the girl just accepted H*ow things work.*

She bravely refused.

"Don't forget what *Mister Sam* also said, Professor. 'I am not for sale!'"

"Yes, yes, I guess I should've known a noble, innocent creature like you isn't for sale," mused Dr. Hardwick, nostalgic. "After all, you're a virgin. One, whose name means: 'most honorable one.' You could just as well be called Mary, Joan, or Therese! Sam Rayburn would've been so proud of you, Dear. He'd have rocked you on his lap, told you a pretty story, let you wear his Stetson, shown you-off to his buddies Harry and Lyndon. '*Mister Sam* was a great soul. His likes will never grace the earth again.' I didn't say that, Churchill did. This is a time when America needs *Mister Sam* more than ever. Unfortunately, like all incomparable statesmen, he's no longer around."

The Professor gave Ashraf an affectionate pat on her unblemished right cheek.

He stroked the girl's long, thick, wavy, jet-black hair.

At first, nothing changed for Ashraf within the cool, quiet, restful, limestone confines of her cloistered section of the university–a structure built three centuries earlier as a precise replica of the school founder's favorite Medieval French monastery in south-central France. For two weeks, life within this clubby, affable, coed academic convent remained as mentally, spiritually fulfilling as before. Like herself, all the Order's sister and brother novices continued professing equal daily devotion to their same noble calling, common lofty cerebral vocation. Ashraf suffered no immediate retribution for her refusal. Never good at catching the point of elaborate amusing anecdotes, she even wondered if perhaps Dr. Hardwick was merely joking.

After a month, however, Ashraf detected a vague, invisible, as solid and recognizable as it also impossible to define storm cloud of official, group disapproval collecting over her idealistic, virginal head. This steadily darkening, malicious, predatory haze pursued the young scholar along every stairway, across each public space or dorm room. It followed the teenager down countless individual walkways. Even professors and grad students from entirely different sections of the campus had no trouble perceiving the changed situation. Until recent weeks her university's precious darling, her school's cherished mascot, the department's beloved prodigy, Miss Kermanshani was now suddenly out of favor.

Soon, too, she was informed that the learned quarterlies no longer wished to publish her articles. Outside conferences abruptly ceased inviting "this singular kid" to speak. All offers of future teaching positions, including at her former undergraduate women's college, evaporated. Scholars once so eager to freely chat or listen at length to Ashraf's latest theories now became forever "previously engaged" or "summoned away" from campus on "urgent family business." Their secretaries always put the youngster's telephone calls on hold. Mail she sent to members of the faculty became invariably: "lost" or "misplaced." All those classes and seminars Ashraf was earlier allowed avoiding suddenly needed to be made up.

Emotional pressure steadily grew.

Ashraf felt isolated, frightened.

Her research work suffered.

She received suspicious, unsettling glances.

Found herself the subject of cruel, snide, easily-audible gossip.

Ashraf's immensely creative mind intimidating to most boys. She possessed no romantic companion in whom she might confide or seek protection. The girl soon developed insomnia, and when at last managing to fall unconscious near morning from sheer exhaustion, she often experienced nightmares or disturbing anxiety dreams. It was a lot to bear, especially for someone who, no matter how gifted and intelligent she might be, was, outside her conservative, paternalistic family and secluded academic environment, just a child.

Even now, return to the fold appeared possible. All might yet be forgiven. The university establishment might still be prepared to dismiss Ashraf's initial opposition as: "naiveté," "schoolgirl impetuosity," "youthful impulsiveness."

She began to panic.

Only one week more of this ostracism, of this, being placed *in-Coventry*, and she would have broken down—begged for clemency, humbly pleaded she be accepted back as "a proper young lady," as "a loyal assistant," a faithful team player cognizant "of how things operate in the adult world."

Such humiliation was only prevented when Ashraf opened the latest issue of her favorite mathematics periodical, next day. Inside, extensively promoted as the journal's "groundbreaking," "crucial," "historic" front article, was a somewhat reworded version of her own most recent paper with its authorship attributed to Dr. Hardwick.

Stunned, angered, insulted but not surprised given the harsh treatment she was meted out in recent weeks, Ashraf telephoned Golbihar, whose celebrity provided easy access to the press.

"If that bastard simply waited a few days more, I'd have broken down and given it to him, anyway!" growled Ashraf, punching the telephone numbers, feeling a great burden lifted from her chest. "I guess he also had second thoughts about letting me drive his *Ferrari*! Likely too, he doesn't enjoy the idea of one day addressing me as 'Professor!' Well, I'll show him! The rotten son-of-a-bitch! I am not going quietly! "

"Next time," she vowed, "that dickhead loser will know to have patience! He is going to regret this!"

The reaction was more violent, ruthless than this girl ever expected.

Almost from the moment Miss Kermanshani publicly accused Dr. Hardwick of plagiarism, of "stealing my own work," all twelve tribes of the university's *Chosen People* rushed to defend one of their own. Since the international media was covering the scandal initially, both the honor of the university and, more importantly, its ready access to near-unlimited state and federal grants, to a vast private organization and wealthy alumni funding, were seen as placed in serious jeopardy. Words heard on television and radio, claims appearing on the internet, stories read in newspapers and magazines, jokes quipped by stand-up comics soon got really nasty.

As in many sexual harassment cases, the victim was portrayed as the criminal, the hunter drawn as his quarry's dupe. The one who suffered was put on trial by her attacker. Ashraf was described to a voyeuristic media ever delighted to unearth dirt in high places, as "a lying, scheming, gold-digging seductress." Dr. Hardwick, so his attorney argued, was at worst: "someone who should have known better." Monday: the tabernacle's cherished pet, the hierarchy's incomparable darling, her order's brilliant cutie, Ashraf was on Friday: the tribe's *Delilah, Jezebel, Potiphar's Wife*.

Even worse followed.

If living in the United States since age six, she becomes a citizen, and she only returned to Iran once. Ashraf was now accused of being an illegal alien, a Shiite fanatic. Her name, it was widely rumored, could be found on the *McCarran-Walter Act* list of foreign subversives either to be deported or denied an entry visa. Anonymous sources even asserted Ashraf belonged to a terrorist sleeper-cell, that she was a member of the Iranian Revolutionary Guard.

"Send her back!" crowds cried. "Send her back!"

The vehemence of such baseless personal attacks and bigoted innuendos suggests that the faculty either came to believe its own propaganda or never considered the girl anything more than an exotic toy or convenient fundraising prop. One, to be safely discarded the moment she ceased being useful to advancing her mentors' own ambitions.

"Send her back! Send her back!"

Shy; modest; raised to always defer to men, never to challenge her elders–Ashraf was totally unprepared for the vicious, concerted, verbal, and written assaults leveled by individuals she regarded just days earlier as wise, kind, encouraging, father-figures. After responding to the attacks by presenting reporters with dated copies of her original notes and first drafts of her papers, she fled to Golbihar's house in Amherst, locked herself in her room, climbed into bed, pulled the covers over her head, and waited for the wrath to subside.

Ashraf never returned to campus. Later, Dr. Hardwick received a Nobel Prize in recognition for being "one of the chief architects of modern advanced mathematics."

If that *Brainy Arab Kid's* most critical accomplishments (Iranians are not Arabs) could be so successfully stolen, it appeared only logical the rest of Ashraf's work would be easy pickings. Various other professors abruptly remembered they being responsible for authoring their famous student's earlier mathematical concepts. If these additional papers were not quite Nobel Prize-level too, they were still good enough to make the alleged true author a college president, the director of a *Think Tank* or a nonprofit fund, be selected as a *PBS, CNN, FOX* Talking-Head, or to be selected as leader of a White *House Blue Ribbon Panel*.

In a matter of just weeks, Ashraf saw all her intellectual achievements piously-filched, the high-brow thieves even demanding written apologies as they blithely destroyed the youngster's career. The "illegal alien," "Iranian spy," "Arab suicide-bomber," "outside agitator," "member of a terrorist cell," was denounced too, as a "slut," a "tart," a "liar," a "fraud," as: "*one of that type*." The college from which she obtained her Bachelor's degree even launched an investigation into the validity of their former student's celebrated undergrad record. After all, **"Girls aren't good at math."**

Ashraf was expelled from the university for plagiarism. Unable to complete her doctorate, she was also blackballed by all the major circles in her discipline.

Human nature being what it is, the public greedily accepted all the false accusations, even inventing a few additional lurid details. There was even talk of turning the event into a movie or a television drama. Still, despite all the: "crisis in youthful values," "soul-searching," "is America in moral decline?" furor traumatizing the entire university town for a month, briefly, too, it captured the avid interest of TV viewers, *Email* correspondents, *Facebook* users, Internet blogs, *Twitter* and *Instagram* followers across the entire country–a year later, no one outside advanced mathematics could remember that the unfortunate affair and its principal character ever occurred, existed.

MR. VILLERS

ONE WINTER AFTERNOON THREE YEARS later in a different state, while she was teaching mathematics at a girls' boarding school, Ashraf went out upon a frozen lake.

"Bravo! Bravo!" cried the delighted onlookers. "Splendid! Splendid!"

If not a multiple Olympic gold-medalist like Golbihar, her little sister could still also give quite a notable performance atop the ice.

In addition, she looked so cute in short, pink ladies figure skating outfit.

One of those applauding the skater was a learned, chivalric, older gentleman from Australia. The two struck up a conversation. Before long, an exchange beginning as idle *Chit-Chat* gravitated into a more severe and rewarding discussion. Later, Mr. Villers invited his new, pretty young friend to dinner.

Ashraf considered for a moment.

Should she accept?

The cloudless heavens were a brilliant sapphire.

Ivory stars appeared in vivid, beckoning constellations.

The Big Dipper, Pegasus, Taurus, Cetus, Hydrus, Andromeda, Perseus, Delphinus

Something about the courtly, traditional, protective manner of Mr. Villers was immediate to Ashraf's liking. A historian who spent his entire adult life writing books on Medieval Europe, he spoke of Eleanor of Aquitaine, Blanche of Castile, Marie de France, St. Francis, Christine de Pizan and Dante as though they were longtime chums. More than a few of that period's best cultural aspects clearly rubbed off on his personality. If anything, the gentleman would make stimulating conversation.

She accepted the invitation.

When Mr. Villers invited Ashraf to a restaurant again the following week, she now readily agreed, as she also did the week after that. Each evening, Mr. Villers insisted on helping his young guest with her chair and coat. He considered it his "obligation" to do the ordering, to snatch up the check before the lady could even look at it. "Don't worry, Miss Kermanshani," he would explain, "the check is always the gentleman's responsibility."

While increasingly longer and more spontaneous, the conversations first at the frozen lake and later over dinner remained somewhat formalized. Mr. Villers, politely steering talk away from subjects he judged inappropriate for his guest's tender years and definite lack of worldly experience. Discussion, he politely restricted to current events, history, literature, and art.

The courtly gentleman admired *Gothic* cathedrals. The young lady, a mathematician, eagerly described the geometrical formulas Medieval architects employed so that these heroically-leaping structures might both be erected and still remain standing proudly over six hundred years later without the use of modern construction materials or techniques. "As in all aspects of life, Mr. Villers," explained Ashraf, "everything ultimately comes down to achieving a balance between conflicting forces."

Host and guest, each, also dearly enjoyed reading *The Romance of Tristan and Iseult*. Ashraf pointed out that, unlike the ancient *Iliad* in which the fight over Helen is a property dispute, the later story from the Twelfth Century is the first significant piece of Western literature concerning romantic love.

Beyond enjoying small-talk, the couple also felt the rapid growth of a more profound mutual attachment, one so evident it required no direct acknowledgment.

"Remember how *Tristan and Iseult* conclude, Miss Kermanshani?"

"Oh yes indeed, Mr. Villers. It's so touching."

"So bad it is the precise name of the author is lost forever.'"

"Beautiful flowering vines grow out from both the lovers' graves and unite."

"Then, people cut the vines down next morning."

"But these beautiful flowering vines join the following night again."

"Then people sever the beautiful flowering vines yet again, Miss Kermanshani."

"But after the beautiful flowering vines unite the graves yet a third time, King Mark orders that no one further interfere, Mr. Villers."

"And so the lovers Tristan and Iseult remain as one to this very day."

"Yes, Mr. Villers, the love that's meant to be, the poet tells us, is the love that's meant to be."

"Maybe one day, Miss Kermanshani, if you wish, seeing where the story is supposed to have occurred, I can show you. It's a most moving, dramatic sight. It's hardly changed in some ways since Tristan and Iseult's' time."

"That sounds like a beautiful spot, Mr. Villers. Perhaps one day, I might take you up on the proposal."

After only a month, Ashraf received an offer of marriage.

Lonely, without friends her age to provide emotional support, a brilliant, possibly historic career lost, she deeply wounded by her betrayal and humiliation at the university–Ashraf found this chivalric, older gentleman exactly the wise, paternal guardian she craved.

The offer of marriage was promptly accepted.

The next three years were the happiest in Ashraf's life.

Although they never actually got around to establishing a formal, legal union, the couple considered themselves wed, all the same. Other people always addressed Ashraf as "Mrs. Villers," and she never once doubted herself to be *Mrs. Villers.* Her husband might be a wealthy man, but he provided his young common-law wife far more than material comfort. He gave Ashraf all his protective, cherishing, nurturing affection. Their bond of mutual concern, the spiritual union, only became deeper, stronger as time passed. Her slightest wish, declared Mr. Villers, was his command. "A gentleman," he explained, "is always of assistance to the ladies."

On days when she requiring no assistance, Ashraf felt obliged to hastily think up a task for her dedicated, faithful knight to perform eagerly. At first, playing *Miss Helpless, Miss Frivolous,* made Ashraf embarrassed, a little ashamed. It made her question if she was taking advantage of such a truly noble spirit. Finally, however, she realized the best way to demonstrate her love, regard, appreciation for him, to enable Mr. Villers to show his own in return, was through consenting to all his courtly, *Old Fashion*, well-meant intervention.

When Ashraf delivered prematurely after only seven months of pregnancy, and her baby lived just ten days, Mr. Villers hardly left his wife's side afterward for a week. He cried as much as she for the loss. He provided their only child—Rebecca–a grave with a lovely white stone marker situated under chestnut trees in a cheerful, *Capability-*Brown *English Style* garden. He also assured the spot was well-tended and regularly supplied fresh flowers.

Tiny Rebecca Villers lived on vividly in both her parents' loving remembrance and active daily consciousness. Their daughter was forever "Our little girl" in the *Present Tense*. The natural passage of time and hectic human events did nothing to diminish this affection. Never was the child to recede from bold recollection and active thought. She wasn't fated like most children dying in infancy to decline into a vague, increasingly forgotten spirit. One, whose memory is revived if at all, and then just briefly, during chance ramblings through yellowing old photographs in dusty scrapbooks. Far from it!

If invisible, unheard to other human eyes and ears, Tiny Rebecca always remained at her parents' side. Not merely did she still comfort them, her steady presence served to encourage doting mother and father to continue fighting for the better world adults each wish for the next generation. A few short days of life are more than enough to secure a lasting emotional link between parent and child.

Mr. Villers took Ashraf to live with him in beautiful stately homes in different countries. In: France, Germany, Switzerland, Spain, Italy, Greece. When Golbihar won an unprecedented third consecutive gold medal at Ladies' Figure Skating, now at the Copenhagen *Winter Olympics,* her younger sister and companion were also here to fondly enjoy this historic triumph.

The chivalric gentleman guided his young gifted, inquiring protégée on trips to fascinating, faraway places she'd previously only learned about from books or seen in movies. He introduced the girl to his noteworthy literary and artistic chums. He enabled *The Dear* to collect paintings, even acquire a Berthe Morisot, and André Derain and a Marie Laurencin. On a trip to Britain, he arranged for Ashraf to be painted nude by David Hockney.

Mr. Villers insisted that Ashraf possess only the most expensive and loveliest dresses, coats, heels, gloves, chapeaus, that she wears only the most exotic hose and lingerie. The husband-father also constructed for his wife-daughter a private indoor skating rink. After the *Brilliant Sweetie* expressed interest in the heavenly bodies, her guardian provided her a huge telescope.

Several times each day without fail, whether at home or abroad, Mr. Villers abruptly took Ashraf in his arms, held her close, covered her with tender kisses before assuring her yet once more of his heartfelt shielding, protective love. He repeated his pledges not only in hopes of pleasing her but for the sheer enjoyment he received voicing them. Eventually, his wife became concerned her husband might injure his back and asked him to desist. Now and again, so, as not to make his *Gifted Young Sweetheart* upset, he partially complied.

While confessing to "understanding not the slightest jot about mathematics," Mr. Villers nevertheless loved to repeatedly hear Ashraf describe all the intricate details of her lofty theories. On this particular occasion, she did so while wearing the latest dress he purchased for her in Paris. "I've no idea what that all those scratchings on the blackboard signify, *Dear*," he commented after his scholarly young wife finished her latest exposition. "But whatever all those wiggly, complicated jottings mean, I'm sure they are important!"

Ashraf tried to repay her guardian by serving as his private secretary and fact-checker as a researcher for his continuing authorship of new penetrating books and journal articles on Medieval history (all of which he dedicated to her). Yet, as eager as she was to help as much as possible, Mr. Villers tended to give her only small assignments.

"I don't want to tire you with my petty concerns, Sweetheart," he explained. "Your head was meant to devote itself to far loftier matters than my own."

Consoling Ashraf once about the sad events at the university, Mr. Villers advised paternally, "Well, God still knows who wrote those papers! And if God knows the truth, if God appreciates the full significance of those papers you wrote, no one else's opinion counts for much in comparison, does it?"

One late afternoon, Mr. Villers abruptly took Ashraf by the hand, leading her upstairs to see the large private study he just ordered constructed for the exclusive "mental labor" his *Pretty, Well-Behaved, Genius.* Bookshelves running from dark wood floors to high molded, fresco ceilings encompassed the length of three of the room's four walls. They were stacked with hundreds, more likely thousands, of books (classics and contemporary works) all related to his companion's subject.

In addition, her protector supplied Ashraf with stacks of the most up-to-date learned periodicals (lifetime subscriptions obtained). Besides a blackboard, a huge antique mahogany desk, and high-backed leather armchair, he also supplied boxes of pens and pencils, a mountain of yellow notepads. Strong lighting was set up so the room's gifted occupant wouldn't strain her eyes. Cork was placed in all the walls to keep out disturbing distracting noise; the bay window looked out upon what Mr. Villers considered: "an inspiring view." Such extra visual niceties provided in a room are always good," he insisted, for "aiding the productive mental juices."

All this was brought together, Mr. Villers elaborated because he worried Ashraf might stifle her intellectual creativity if, like Virginia Woolf, she was unable "to find peace and refuge in a quiet, fitting for her abilities, intellectual temple all of her own." Here, undisturbed among her books, journals and papers, Mr. Villers was confident, his *"Far Over My Head Little Girl"* would soon develop even further mathematical concepts her protector couldn't understand.

"I'll certainly try my best, Mr. Villers," replied Ashraf, humble, deeply grateful, immensely honored, by companion's constant attention and encouragement of her mathematics. "I hope I can produce something new for you, Mr. Villers."

"I'm confident you will, *Dear*," he guaranteed. "I know my wife can certainly produce!"

The gentleman himself short. He and begged forgiveness if his comment was interpreted the wrong way.

"No, no, Mr. Villers," reassured Ashraf. "I didn't at all interpret what you said the wrong way!"

His wife always addressed her husband by his surname. She believed it wasn't anywhere near her place calling him Robertson, especially not *Bob*. It was pretty presumptuous, she thought, being on a first-name basis with such a wise master. If some visitors thought this manner of addressing a spouse affected or self-demeaning, Ashraf didn't think so. To her, polite formality was only appropriate. It was as well, a tender expression of her grateful love. The idea of possessing an intimate companion deserving of immense deference, allegiance, and respect she found extremely comforting, warming, reassuring. It gave her confidence she was cherished, nurtured, and, above all, protected.

These were the three happiest years in her life—three years precisely.

On the day following the anniversary, Mr. Villers instructed Ashraf to sit on his lap, clutching his left arm firm, and lean her head on her guardian's shoulder.

"Sweetheart, I won't be able to take care of you much longer," explained Mr. Villers paternally, running his right hand through companion's long, thick, sinuous, black hair, kissing her on the forehead. "I won't be able much longer to listen to all those far-over-my-head concepts. However, I've seen to the matter and made sure that whatever happens in the future, you'll be well provided for. You'll never be compelled to desert your blessed mathematics. A gentleman is of assistance to the ladies. It's been my special and never once dared imagine privilege, to be of service, to one particular damsel."

Ashraf burst into frantic tears.

Ever the gentleman, he duty-bound to assist the ladies, Mr. Villers dried his wife's tears with a long silk handkerchief. Wishing she not be overly distraught at the news, he suggested the two now take a stroll across the estate.

"Come with me," he said, rising from a *Queen Anne Style* chair. Ashraf, still clutching her protector's arm tight, was lifted to her own feet in the same motion. "I won't be dead next week, Sweetheart. I've still got a little energy remaining in me. Why don't we go and take a walk in the garden and visit our daughter?"

"Oh yes, indeed Mr, Villers. Please take me for a walk in the garden so we can visit Rebecca. You won't be leaving me next week."

I

Six months later, only days after Mr. Villers died, his relatives (none of whom came for a visit during his lifetime or attended his funeral), either in person or through attorneys, transmitted the young widow legal papers.

Ashraf's late husband possessed four siblings along with an army of cousins, nieces, nephews, and grasping in-laws. There too, surfaced an alleged former Mrs. *Villers*, claiming to be cheated in the purported earlier couple's divorce settlement. Additionally, popping out of the woodwork were three heretofore completely unknown or unrecorded teenage mothers, each one asserting Mr. Villers fathered her child. Besides blood or supposed-blood family come to serve notice, there also arrived an *Old Flame* charging breach-of-promise, a college chum to whom Mr. Villers once made idle pledges, a landscape architect, a used-car dealer, an estate manager, a Protestant minister desirous of funds to build a new wing on his Mega-church; even a man declaring he and Mr. Villers had a same-sex marriage!

All these vultures were anxious with varying-degrees of pious self-promotion, to either: "receive what was solemnly promised me long ago;" to: "save the estate for those who truly loved, appreciated the dear, scholarly gentleman;" or: "to keep poor Uncle Bob's fortune out of the hands of that underhanded-Iranian, college drop-out, publicity-seeking *WOG* who only got herself pregnant so she'd be able to put her hands on the gullible old guy's money." It was, these previously unknown claimants asserted, a stereotypical case of a wealthy, feeble-minded but still sexually-aroused elder man seduced by a pretty gold-digger less than half his age. After all, "there's no fool like an old fool."

Following three years of relying implicitly on Mr. Villers to make all the decisions, she instinctively trusting in Mr. Villers to do what was best for her, regarding him from the outset as her father no less than her husband–Ashraf was will-prepared for confronting this onslaught. Her area of expertise was mathematics and, to a lesser degree, literature. She knew as much about estate law as the dark side of the moon! She understood legal tomes no better than cuneiform tablets! Her only vague conception of the rules governing property was gleaned from Jane Austen, Dickens, and Balzac novels where blood-connection, no matter how distant, is the ultimate factor determining ownership. From this perspective, the situation wasn't at all promising.

If she bequeathed her companion's entire financial fortune, material possessions, and land holdings, their common-law union-made Ashraf in the eyes of the court, only Mr. Villers' much younger and relatively recent acquired concubine. Economically-dependent never worked, no significant savings of her own, she at no time contributed to her protector's estate. Nearly everything the couple acquired was purchased with Mr. Villers' money, registered under his name. Additionally, there was no cute baby in a weeping young Mama's arms to draw sympathy or employ as negotiating tool. The Villers family also made much of "that Iranian slut's" reputation as a "Muslim terrorist," "college plagiarizer," "illegal alien," to imply the current will was undoubtedly counterfeit.

Estate law has considerably evolved since the days of Jane Austen, Dickens, and Balzac; a contemporary judge would have thrown out all the challenges in five minutes. Today in the United States, an unmarried man of sound mind is free bequeathing all his property to Vladimir Putin if he so wishes. The Villers's relatives and the other fortune-hunters knew this. However, they were confident of getting what they wanted without ever going to court.

Following only a few additional days of hectoring attorneys, harassing unannounced visits, and politely threatening telephone calls, Ashraf panicked. In exchange for a written, notarized assurance that the bullies would never challenge her possession of the couple's house in Amherst, Massachusetts, she signed away almost everything. It was all too reminiscent of Ashraf's earlier experience at the university.

Mr. Villers, though, remained true to his pledge. His wife was "to be provided for," she never compelled to abandon her "blessed mathematics." Like the eternal vine of love uniting Tristan and Iseult, this other example of affection, too, could not be severed even through death. Possibly anticipating exactly what transpired upon his passing, Mr. Villers established a separate well-invested, well-managed investment account guaranteed to assure *My Little Scholar* a fine annual income for the rest of her life. This separate investment account was placed outside his companion's control and thus her authority to give it away. If this arrangement was old-fashion, some argued paternalistically, Mr. Villers was an old-fashion, paternalistic individual.

Following receipt of a second written, notarized letter, this one guaranteeing that her daughter's grave in the garden would always be cared-for, Ashraf rented out the house in Amherst, Massachusetts and moved to Paris, France. Only rarely did she return to the United States. And then, only to see Rebecca's grave and to visit her sister Golbihar, the great Olympic figure skater.

II

Mrs. Robertson Villers (no one in France knew *Ashraf Kermanshani* ever existed) slowly recovered the assertiveness of her adolescence, college, and first university years. She gradually regained the idealistic bravery for which even Dr. James Hardwick conceded admiration. It was this personal quality, for which, he said, Sam Rayburn would have placed the girl on his lap, let her wear his stetson, told her a pretty story, showed her off to his chums Harry and Lyndon.

She again began publishing papers on advanced mathematics, now under her married name.

During one pensive afternoon strolling in the **Pascale Kedari Memorial Garden**, Mrs. Villers developed a fascination with large, entangled vines. Two huge, flowering separate entities, which, no matter how often they were pruned-back, swift, like those beside the tombs of Tristan and Iseult, reunite as a single being. A second visit led to a third. On her fourth, she came to bury Mr. Villers' ashes. She, preparing a spot just beside, where his wife planned at some later date to also be interred. As in the great Medieval love saga, she arranged so that the couple might, at last, reunite in a warm embrace for all eternity.

By the end of the year, the American expatriate's deep concern for the little park won her an invitation to join the executive board of the *Ladies Garden Trust*.

Considering their separate life experiences, it was almost inevitable that Mrs. Villers and Countess de Montfort should develop a mutual dislike. So unfortunate it was the pair were not better acquainted. If they were given that chance, one would show herself to be far from simply a self-absorbed *Angry Woman*, and the other, demonstrate she infinitely more than just the bed-partner of influential males. The two ladies possessed a further bond from which lasting friendship might spring. If male-dominated society barred Ashraf her choice of career, it kept Celine from knowing that choice for a woman even exists.

END OF PART I

SUCCESSION CRISIS

"THERE! FINISHED! DONE AT LAST!" pronounced Countess de Montfort gleefully, her long cherry blond hair fallen over pretty face. The picture-recording expedition through her beloved green space running parallels the Right embankment was, at last, complete. For these historic grounds and their proper upkeep, best maintenance, she felt almost the same deep, emotional responsibility as does a mother for a small child. Her melodic voice expressed both rightful pride at a task well done and delight with yet further demonstrating her recently discovered a gift for photography. "I'm finished at last! As my two little girls would say if they were here watching me: 'Mama, that was— Awesome, *really*— awesome!"

Some of the phonographs Celine took that afternoon in the **Pascale Kedari Memorial Garden** rank among the best of her entire career. Three of the camera shots won greatly-coveted international artistic prizes. A fourth is found currently on a French postage stamp; a fifth is well-known from its appearance on posters advocating environmental causes; a sixth is equally familiar to the General Public thanks to the image's selection to represent a major world diplomatic event held at the United Nations. The complete series of brilliant, thought-provoking color pictures was published in a prestigious, award-winning, critically-acclaimed book. Going into many succeeding editions and available for sale throughout most of the world, Countess de Montfort's celebration of nature's beauty still remains in print today.

I

In final preparation for the emergency meeting of the *Ladies Garden Trust,* she called for tomorrow over luncheon, Countess de Montfort decorated all four papered walls of her townhouse's elegant dining hall with copies of her favorite new 8-by-10 inch color glossies.

Each image finely recorded a different section of the famous verdant enclosure running parallel to the Right embankment.

"There you are!" exclaimed the fetching camera-lady to herself in **Third Person** upon completing decorations. "That's a good job you've done! Those are some good photo-shots indeed!"

"Ooh!" cried the Countess, her lovely bare arms with hands in fists reaching well above head in imitation of a General de Gaulle bodily V-for-victory shape. "Ooh! Ooh! Yes, *ooh!*"

Celine had not experienced such well-earned-elation. She felt such a high sense of honorable pride, been possessed of so clear a knowledge of achieving a noble, valuable, worthwhile accomplishment since she is wearing knee socks.

She giggled.

She giggled again.

Next, she took off her heels.

After first determining that no one else was watching, Celine began to circumnavigate the great dining hall with its oak waxed floor and twelve meter-high. Watteau frescoed-ceiling with neoclassical moldings.

She adopted a carefree, triumphant, girlish skip.

First only humming the tune, she soon joyously sang the words of her favorite Bob Dylan ballad.

"Hey, Mr. Tambourine Man, play a song for me–"

Once around the hall, Celine traveled in song.

"–And now that evening's empire has vanished into sand–"

A second time around, she traveled at skip, her melodic voice echoing.

For yet a third circumnavigation, she journeyed musically, at merry kip.

"–In that jingle, jangle morning, I'll keep following you."

In time, catching the attention of Celine's deep green eyes, beneath the portrait of an earlier Montfort Lady painted by Reynolds was a marble-top, waxed, *Queen Anne* walnut chest-of-drawers with shined-brass shelf handles. Atop this piece of furniture stood a large, gilt-framed, studio photograph of the previous Countess de Montfort— she, also named Marie-Therese-Celine. The last Countess wore a strapless, white, silk opera gown. Strings of Hapsburg and Bourbon Era natural pearls and solid gold Carolingian crucifix decorated this lady's graceful neck, bare shoulders and arms, quite visible bosom. A tiara of red, blue, and green *Gupta Period* Indian diamonds crowned her head with long, thick, cherry blond hair. Matchless Romanov emeralds were on her ears, Capetian and Hohenstaufen stones on her small, sculpted hands. Two fabulously-jeweled Byzantine gold bracelets first given to Theodora by Justinian, then passed on to Catherine the Great by Prince Potemkin now celebrated this later noble dames' delicate wrists.

Newcomers observing the photograph would easily assume it to be the image of a monarch. Indeed, except for the two's difference in hair color, this previous Countess de Montfort possessed a striking resemblance to Great Britain's Danish *La Belle Époque* queen, Alexandra.

In truth, richer, deeper, older (if admitted illegitimate) royal blood circulates through the Montfort clan's veins than is found in all the other European monarchies put together. The gilt-framed studio photograph atop the antique chest-of-drawers was taken just a month before this earlier grand courtesan was killed at age only thirty-four in a skiing accident at the family's estate on Mt. Anne. Thus, frozen in time, she remains eternally young, forever beautiful.

This earlier Countess's three children, seated just beside her in the picture, ages: twelve (in white dress); ten (in lapis-lazuli dress) and eight; (tangerine), clearly inherited their mother's imperious, commanding, authoritarian loveliness. Not surprisingly, it was from her tragic mother that the eldest daughter acquired a habit for describing her charming progeny as—"All my best genes, all, my best *DNA!*"

Celine halted to contemplate the photograph. Especially to meditate upon the image it included of her own earlier, miniature self. With a chest displaying the arrival of puberty, her long cherry blond hair tied-back in the hope of looking older, she was attempting Churchillian resolve on the cute, virginal face. The twelve-year-old wished to look "grown-up" for the camera. She wanted to appear "a proper young lady." Simultaneously, the girl failed, noticing that her knee socks were drooped to ankles and the buckle of her left flat shoe was come unfastened.

"Precious! Priceless!" mused the image's current adult counterpart, with tender, nostalgic voice and smile, "Oh, if, life all just remained that, way, never changed!"

Further observation of the photograph evoked less happy thoughts. The twelve-year-old clutched her regal parent's left arm tightly as if she feared Mama was lost should a child ever let her go.

"Maybe I had a premonition of what was soon to come?" pondered Celine.

She crossed herself.

Recited a devotional prayer.

Lifted the gilt-framed photograph with both hands.

Kissed the picture of her mother, fervent.

As if her lips were applied to a holy, magical Russian icon.

"I still love you so much, Mama" the parent's eldest daughter pledged in a choked voice, hair in face, tears obscuring her vision. "I always will! I love you so much, Mama! So-so-so much! The only reason I didn't name one of my own girls for you is that I was frightened that might make her die as you died. I'm sure you'll understand."

"You know, Mama," her daughter, now grown up, continued, "I try to love you as you love me! I know you're in a better place today. Still, I can't help feeling lonely and unsure without you to care for me, to give me courage! I'm sorry if that's selfish. Please forgive me if it is. I don't mean it to be selfish."

Celine again kissed the photograph as if it were a holy, magical Russian icon.

In fact, unlike her reverent eldest daughter, Mama, Countess Marie de Montfort–known to those who loved her as *Countess Manon*–had been an avowed agnostic. She permitted her children to be baptized,

54

taught catechism and confirmed in the Roman Catholic Church simply out of family tradition.

"I believe religion is just a lot of Dark Ages, witchdoctor, mumbo-jumbo," Countess Manon confided to a gentleman chum while she merrily, teary-eyed, snapping endless photos of Celine and Philippine at the church altar, each child wearing a frilly, white, first communion dress. "But through me denying my girls an opportunity deciding for themselves" their parent added philosophically, "I'll be just preaching another form of Dark Ages, witchdoctor mumbo-jumbo!" If her oldest child's devotion to the Virgin was an entirely personal conviction, there is no doubt how this more spiritual offspring visualized that ethereal figure.

Adult Celine crossed herself again.

She next set the gilt-framed studio photograph back atop the *Queen Anne* chest-of-drawers with shining brash shelf handles.

Today's Celine adjusted her short, chartreuse dress, fiddled with the religious medal around her slender neck. A moment later, she resumed her multiple-circumnavigations of the great hall. This time, she moved silently and at a slow, reflective, measured step.

"Poor Mama."

If given the freedom and opportunity to do so, Countess Manon might well have led the *Warsaw Rising,* been the discoverer of the source of the Nile, she scaled *Mt. Everest* "because it's there," or composed a famous violin concerto in *D-Major.* If provided the chance, this lady might too have delivered a historic radio broadcast from London on June 18, 1940, deciphered *Hieroglyphics,* been the architect of Chartres, the creator of the windows of Sainte Chapelle, or, perhaps, she, even also written a matchless, timeless diary preserved after its author's betrayal to the Nazis. Within a social environment severely limiting her independence of action, however, Countess Manon found no choice but to restrict her dynamism within the gilded cage she was so luxuriously but forever confined.

Countess Manon decided she wished to be an *enlightened, forward-looking, innovative mother*. Parenting books from the United States, she read during her first pregnancy, convinced her of the vital necessity for establishing a—*solid, intimate, enduring, emotional bond*—between mother and child. Rather than employing a strict French, German, or Spanish governess as was the family's long custom, Countess Manon announced the intention of rearing her offspring, personally.

This is the "bold," "brave," "democratic," late-Twentieth Century, she explained to all her more traditionalist female relatives and conservative gentleman chums. Her words promptly leaving listeners speechless, stupefied by their open, daring, unmitigated rupture with haloed precedent. The day for all too-long delayed and essential social transformation was clearly at last, at hand! She advised why this truth was even *Blowing-in-the wind.* "*The times*," she said, "*they are a-changing.*" Everyone of goodwill, was now in a position to play his or even **her** part in advancing this noble cause—even mothers at home with small children!

"Has Manon become a Communist?" pondered aloud her astonished relatives and gentleman chums upon at last recovered their ability to speak.

"Has Manon been seduced into some left-wing cult? Is she preparing to go and fight in the jungle with *Che?* Is she going to start wearing trousers?"

"Could Manon be getting ready to enter one of those American university-drop-out communes?" voiced other society acquaintances with no less closed-minded sincerity. "Is Manon going to teach her daughters to smoke marijuana, take *LSD,* let them cut their hair short, become street protestors! Maybe even let one of them marry a Negro!"

"The torch has been passed to a new generation!'" explained the free-spirited Countess to those preferring this flame continue being situated just where it was. There was commencing, she prophesied, "a time for conquering a *New Frontier.*" A time for opening passageways to heretofore uncharted wondrous new continents! Today was inaugurating "an era to attain the summit of mountaintops climbers have as yet never even dreamed reaching!"

To meet all these epic-challenges, to be *prepared to pay any price, bear any burden*," explained Countess Manon, "children of today not merely require but deserve their parents' frequent, easily-obtained, encouraging, and physically affectionate attention." The age of–the reserved, aloof, frigid, "come give Mummy her weekly kiss and then run-along to governess"-mother–was over! And good riddance, too! The usual upper-class near-feudal relationship between parent and child, so distant, formalized, unloving, was completely revolutionized! "A parent today was not merely her child's legal guardian, but her child's friend."

Rather than just pontificating, however, Countess Manon wished to personally set her isolated, rarefied social class a good example, to offer it great new goals to seize. "Or, to quote Harry Truman: 'At least I'm going to god-damn-well, son-of-a-bitch, try!'"

Countess Manon breastfed all three of her girls—not merely her firstborn and namesake, but also Philippine, then Leonie. In addition, this direct descendant of Charlemagne and Otto the Great changed all her babies' diapers *(Pampers* only just appearing on the market). She proudly wheeled each "princess" down the wide avenues and through the wooded parks of Paris in a pram, brought them with her to garden parties, social events. She flew into rapturous joy whenever passersby stopped to compliment her for bearing such splendid progeny, for possessing such excellent parenting skills.

"Oh, I am simply trying my best to be a good mother, Monsieur!" she responded demurely to one well-wisher in the historic, enclosed garden running parallel the Right embankment. "People have no business bringing children into this troubled, hectic world if they don't intend caring for them as the little dears deserve! Providing them frequent love and attention as is their parents' sacred obligation!"

Countess Manon's decision to be an *enlightened, forward-looking, innovative* mother proved no mere passing upper-class whim. Neither did she act like a pampered chatelaine with a legion of servants doing all the hard work in their mistress's idle fancy. She wasn't Marie Antoinette playing shepherdess at Versailles (the already well-trained, scrubbed-down lambs first set in careful line so Her Majesty need not fear dirtying her soft, aristocratic, white hands). No. Countess Manon was not just— *Slumming-it* or—*Out-to-see-how-the-other-half-lives.*

She constantly bombarded family and friends with boxes of "precious photos." None of her intimates were able to go home until they were first watching the latest jiggling, not fully in focus home movie chronicling *My Little Ones'* "brilliant development." The walls of the front foyer of No. 3 Rue Artemis were covered with framed examples of "my young artists'" crayon scribble. Countess Manon assisted each of her three daughters to toddle her first steps (filming the event), to say the child's first words (recorded on tape), learn to use the potty, dress herself, to fasten the child's own mary-janes. Not merely her firstborn, namesake Celine received such devoted maternal attention but also Philippine Luria and Leonie Golitsyn.

Countess Manon asked the children always to address her as Mama. She frequently offered the comfort of her lap and was more than generous with tender hugs and heartfelt kisses. The little girls were personally escorted in the Montfort clan's black, stretch-limousines to the most exclusive pediatricians. Once there, if young arms or bottoms felt the pinch of doctor's shots, Mama was swift providing consolation, joining children in their tears. Whenever at night, one of her dears suffered a bad dream or felt too cold in her own room, the child was free to climb into Mama's own warm, reassuring canopied bed. On occasion, it got crowded.

Meticulous to avoid sibling rivalry, Countess Manon undertook all possible effort giving each of her daughters an equal share of maternal affection, the same length of time alone with her. When Celine suffered from croup, Mama stayed up all night nursing her at the bedside. As she did too, later for Philippine and then Leonie. Each girl was personally taught by Mama how to read, write in cursive, was inspired by the same attentive parent to develop a deep lifetime interest in literature, the visual arts, and music. The children were each taken to museums and Bob Dylan concerts, on picnics, and when each was old enough to libraries. Mama was ever so fond of parading her progeny about in pretty dresses and tying on alternating days a big red, green, white, or blue bow in each girl's hair. Primary colors were only fitting, she believed, for *primary* children.

When Celine early demonstrated a singular aptitude for the piano, Mama immediately arranged for the talented child to receive lessons from the best teachers in Europe. Philippine and Leonie were given no less distinguished instruction in perfecting their clear artistic gifts for poetry and sculpture. Mama loved all three. The girls were her first and last concern.

As Countess Manon insisted to passersby, "I just want to be a good mother."

Today, cynics might claim there was nothing at all "unique" or "innovative" about Countess Manon's parenting style. In a sense, she was no different from millions of other socially liberal parents of her era. Neither was she by any means the only woman crying when John F. Kennedy was assassinated, nor the sole person knowing by heart the words of Bob Dylan's *Blowing in the Wind; Mr. Tambourine Man, The Times they are a-Changing, Like a Rolling Stone.*

Conversely, as a highly intelligent, talented woman provided no choice but to serve the aristocracy as a courtesan, her eagerness to challenge centuries of tradition made Countess Manon both extraordinary and bold. Within her small, restricted, domestic sphere, she possessed a soul far more revolutionary than many freer individuals commonly described as political or social radicals. One can only imagine how infinitely greater, wider, more lasting an influence Countess Manon's dynamism would exercise upon larger western society was she allowed expressing it there.

And then abruptly, she was gone.

One seemingly unremarkable winter morning at the villa on Mt. Anne, after first giving the children her usual warm kiss, Mama went out as she often did to ski. She promised to return as on all preceding days, to make them lunch. Celine and her sisters possessed no reason to think otherwise. Yet when the door reopened later than expected, it wasn't Mama entering but Auntie Bernarde, a troubled expression on her face.

Countess Manon was so battered and bloodied during the skiing accident, and relatives decided it would be too emotionally difficult for her daughters to view their mother's body. Celine became so distraught upon learning the news, she needed to be sedated and was unable to attend the funeral. For her children, when Countess Manon departed the house to ski that morning, she vanished. She was suddenly taken from them without a trace.

"Poor Mama! She was such a noble creature. She was so much better than all us!" sighed the reigning Countess de Montfort two decades later. "At least, Mama will never grow old."

Setting the gilt-framed photograph back atop the antique chest of drawers, today's adult Celine again meandered nostalgically the vast dining hall of No, 3 Rue Artemis.

Opposite the treasured image of her mother was commemorated one of the Montfort clan's great male relatives (admittedly, an illegitimate one): Prince Louis d'Enghien de Bourbon-Condé—known to history as *The Grand Condé*. The celebrated field marshal ranks second only to Napoleon in the long, vivid annals of distinguished French military command. In a huge, colorful Baroque mural covering the dining hall's entire south wall, Prince d'Enghien was depicted at the Battle of Rocroi—the decisive confrontation of *The Thirty Years War.* He, winning both victories over the Hapsburgs and establishing generations of French military supremacy in Western Europe.

Cardinal Jules Mazarin, the Prince d'Enghien's bitter rival and ultimate nemesis (both in politics and access to the Queen Regent's bed), was portrayed, too. If only for historical accuracy, he could not be omitted totally. Yet in a clear act of out-maneuvered foe's subtle artistic revenge, Mazarin is exiled to the extreme bottom left corner of the vast panorama. At its center, however, instantly catching the attention of all viewers, is the Prince d'Enghien. Here, atop a white rearing charger, bridle reins in right gloved-hand, his left, holding a saber to the cloudless sky, bird-of-paradise feathers flowing from a wide gray hat, he wearing an aquamarine frock coat, cloth-of-gold cordon, frilly white shirt, shin-high black musketeers boots, excruciatingly-tight red breeches–the great field marshal gazes down contemptuously on his less heroic but more politically and sexually adept descendants.

If, as children, Philippine Luria and Leonie Golitsyn much enjoyed taunting, sticking out their tongue, making faces at the vain, pompous horseman, Celine was positively terrified of the life-size painting. Prince d'Enghien's beady eyes, she long thought, followed her own every step, his high-minded facial expression registering sharp disapproval of the little girl's every thought, word, or physical movement. Unlike her older sisters, Celine's ways made sure never to come within six feet of the horseman. Lest, the rider's large saber bring three-hundred-and-fifty-years of personal animosity crashing down on her own tender, young head.

"There was no doubt about it," little Celine was convinced. That nasty warrior is eagerly waiting for the slightest opportunity to strike her! That he was painted by Georges de la Tour made the Prince d'Enghien and his colorful, vivid panorama no less dreadful. The image entered all Celine's childhood nightmares. If others only feared confronting the *Bogeyman*, she told friends, "I have actually met the monster!"

And worse still, the fiend was a relative who lived in her house!

"Mama, Mama! Mama! That means Prince d'Enghien is after me, again!" cried out Celine on more than a few dark nights. "He's really after me this time, Mama!"

"Don't be scared, Dear," assured Countess Manon, comforting her eldest daughter on the last such distressing, upsetting occasion. "You can come and sleep with me for the rest of the night! Soon you'll discover the Prince is such a coward, and he can only come out at night. And even then, he's so scared of little girls he runs away the first time he finds they've recognized him. Soon, if not perhaps even already tonight, the Prince is going to conclude it's far safer for a timid character like him to stay where he is and never prowl again—I, promise, Dear!"

Just as Countess Manon guaranteed, the Prince d'Enghien never again revealed his nasty presence in Celine's bedroom. Soon, she even joined Philippine and Leonie in making faces at the ogre in his *Seventeenth-Century* high-brow propaganda picture. "Watch who's coming for you!

Watch who's coming for you!" all three sisters teased, each motioning with her own little right forefingers to remind the Prince of his un-doer approaching from the mural's far bottom left.

"Ooh! Nobody can stop Cardinal Mazarin from getting you, you silly man!" Celine called to the rider once so dreadful to her eyes, so frightening in her childhood's thoughts and dreams. Now, thanks to Countess Manon, he becomes only a vain fool. "I'm not scared of you anymore! So I'm not scared to say you look foolish with that long wig and wearing those ever-so-so-so-tight breeches!"

Today's adult Celine now observed a second marble-top, waxed, *Queen Anne* walnut chest-of-drawers with shined brass shelf handles. It was located near the bay window at the center of the chamber's east wall. Atop stood another large gilt-framed studio photograph of a beautiful lady—she, like Countess Manon, could be easily mistaken for a queen, tsarina, or empress.

Niece halted to contemplate her Auntie's image, long and deep.

Like Countess Manon, her no less pretty younger sister Marie-Bernarde-Julienne de Charente, was also a direct descendant of Charlemagne and Otto the Great. In this second formal, gilt-framed photograph, Madame de Charente, too, wore a strapless opera gown, her aquamarine instead of white. She, too, possessed a graceful neck, charming bare shoulders, and arms had a fine and quite visible bosom. If her mounds of thick hair dark brown, not cherry blond, they were no less splendid. In this photograph, taken just a week following her older sister's death, Madame de Charente, however, not Celine, who had succeeded to the *Gupta Period* red, blue, and green diamond tiara. It was Auntie Bernarde, not Celine, who possessed all the other magnificent, museum-piece jewelry. Her niece, once the presumed heiress to the Montfort legacy, did not even appear in this second picture.

Tragic as it was, the brutal early death of Countess Manon also provoked a succession crisis. A sudden, unforeseen leadership vacuum emerged, placing the continuation of the grand courtesan dynasty in terrible jeopardy. For the first time in centuries, the influential clan was without an effective, experienced leader. In past centuries, others, too,

62

holding that position, abruptly departed the scene at a relatively young age.

One, the previous Countess de Montfort, was murdered by a rejected lover.

A second lost her head on the guillotine during *The Reign of Terror*.

If not she died violently, a third earlier Countess de Montfort unexpectedly discovered religion and entered a convent.

Nevertheless, in all three cases, the departed chatelaine left behind an adult natural or adopted daughter already established in her vocation. One, who could either immediately or in short order replace her mother as skilled, successful manager of their unique family business.

In stark contrast, the twelve-year-old with drooped knee socks hoping to make a *grown-up* expression on her unworldly face while desperately gripping Countess Manon's protective arm would not for perhaps a decade be either intellectually or physically prepared to supervise Europe's grandest tribe of grand courtesans. The mere idea was too obscene even to mention! Rather than a Montfort Lady, Celine was still a Montfort *child.* If Auntie Bernarde had not intervened in those unsteady, uncertain days following her older sister's tragic death, a renowned, historic dynasty surely would have sputtered, petered to an inglorious end.

"As much as I love Mama," acknowledged Countess Manon's oldest daughter today, contemplating the second photograph, "I owe even more in my life to Auntie Bernard!" Rather than a *Wicked Stepmother,* she was the orphan's *Good Fairy.*

That was easy to say with the benefit of adult hindsight.

Child and adolescent Celine wasn't at all so sure.

ANDANTE

WHILE COUNTESS MANON WAS KILLED on a Wednesday in the French Alps, her funeral and burial occurred in Paris the following Monday. Both ceremonies were intended to be simple, ecumenical, family gatherings honoring *The Departed*'s fine personal qualities. Nominally Roman Catholic but avowed agnostic, Countess Manon never affiliated with or was active in any parish. Relatives decided it was insulting to her memory to include in the service any liturgy or hymns containing words all knew the lady did not believe. Unfortunately, those never meeting this gentle soul in life transformed the events following her death into a huge, vulgar, public spectacle.

Celine's inability to attend was likely for the twelve-year-old's best.

Her–brutal early death; given-name evoking grand opera; position in the aristocracy; her good looks, idealistic, vulnerable, feminine personality; a sense among the public of she being rejected by her own materialistic kind, of she is a rebel against false, rigid social convention–all these factors persuaded *Twenty-Four-Hour-Seven* international news outlets to portray Countess Manon as another Princess Diana of Wales. Just as the media hoped, their effort was successful. Soon, all television viewers, radio listeners, newspaper readers, *Email* correspondents, *Facebook* devotees, *Internet* blogs, *Instagram, SmartPhone* addicts, and computer chat rooms of either a romantic or voyeuristic temperament became enraptured with this quite tempting if not precisely accurate comparison.

As occurring earlier outside London's Buckingham Palace, the entrance to cream color No. 3 Rue Artemis in Paris was soon blockaded with oceans of reverential flowers. As in August 1997 Britain, government flags across France also were hung at half-mast. Church bells once more intoned mournfully. Politicians, academics, religious leaders, Popstars, sports heroes, celebrities, and ordinary citizens all, each, donned black armbands. Countess Manon's funeral was televised live on all continents, including Antarctica. Legislatures, ministries, embassies, and courts across the planet again solemnly adjourned critical business so their members might not be deprived following events on the TV screen.

The funeral was held at St. Severin, the famous *Romanesque* structure on the Seine's Left Bank. All approaches to the church for several serpentine streets in every direction were flooded by a sea of weeping, writhing mourners. Traffic throughout Paris came to a standstill for hours. Helicopters with television news cameras clogged the air. After the funeral service, during the Snail's Pace-journey to the cemetery in the 20th Arrondissement, fistfights often broke-out, and language highly inappropriate for this sad occasion echoed as contending mobs of grievers fought one another to commandeer the hearse of this second "Candle in the wind."

Snaking at last through weeping humanity, the cortege finally reached *Pere Lachaise Cemetery*. It, already the resting place of such historical-cultural icons as: Abelard and Heloise, Balzac, Chopin, Piaf, Moliere, Colette, Sarah Bernhardt, Daumier, Pissarro, Max Ernst, Benjamin Constant, Ingres, Modigliani, Proust, Rossini, Delacroix, Georges Bizet, Rachel, Isadora Duncan, Marcel Marceau, Simone Signoret, Gericault, David, Michelet, Corot, La Fontaine, Oscar Wilde, Seurat, Richard Wright, Colonel Fabien, Yves Montand, Gertrude Stein and Jim Morrison. Once arrived, however, the body of Countess Manon was nearly mutilated by relics-seekers when her coffin burst open after crashing to the ground as members of rival hysterical crowds tried snatching it from the official pallbearers. Then, two Carmelite nuns and a Franciscan friar, each wishing to be buried alive with "The New Magdalene," first needed to be pulled kicking-and-screaming out of the burial site before the now re-sealed casket could finally be placed in the ground.

During the following year, Countess Manon was the most famous, the most admired, most beloved, and widely-discussed individual on the face of the earth. There was serious talk of turning her life story into either a movie or a *PBS* television series. Famous actresses both in Europe and America fought tooth-and-nail to receive the privilege of portraying her on either the big or small screen. After the passage of twelve months, however, few of the seeming-numberless men and women, boys and girls, once fulsomely pledging their eternal devotion to Countess Manon's memory, to preaching her *Good News*, could still recall the tragic lady's name. Or recollect when, where, why, and exactly how she died. Today, outside her enclosed social milieu and cemetery tourists, Countess Manon is no better remembered than is Ashraf Kermanshani.

The grotesque public spectacle did nothing to hinder secret domestic plans already afoot. By volunteering to stay behind to comfort her heavily-sedated niece, Madame de Charente, from childhood the pet of the house staff, created an ideal situation to stage a palace coup. By the time their relatives squirmed back through the hysterical crowds and congested traffic, a new regime was unexpectedly installed at cream color No. 3 Rue Artemis.

Alone with Celine in the first floor *Louis XV Style*-salon following the mourners' departure for religious services, Madame de Charente, seated elegantly in a cherry wood blue damask armchair, her legs daintily crossed, began reading to the young invalid that morning's edition of *La Croix*. Lying prone on a deep, comfortable white couch beside the girl's head, still groggy from the doctor's sedative injection last night, Celine just vaguely understood the words she heard.

"Isn't that wonderful news, Dear?" asked Madame de Charente in a merry voice upon completion of one of the newspaper's main articles. "Isn't that wonderful to know?"

"Oh, yes, Auntie Bernarde, yes Auntie Bernarde," mumbled Celine. "I, too, think it's wonderful. Bless you, Auntie Bernarde, for telling me the wonderful news."

If not sure exactly what this "wonderful news" constituted, the girl was still cognizant enough to perceive she had heard "wonderful news" of some kind.

Madame de Charente then cast the newspaper aside.

Lifting her ladylike right hand, she gave a prearranged signal.

An instant later, the members of the domestic staff appeared, ready and eager.

"From this moment forward, Jeanne, Félicitée, Andrée, Pierrette, Therese, Yolande," announced Madame de Charente, rising to feet, adjusting her pantyhose, short skirt, and buttons of silk, white blouse."From this moment forward, I am the new Countess de Montfort!"

"Yes, so you are *Missy*!" declared her *Praetorian Guard* in enthusiastic unison. "From this moment forward, our Little Bernie is the new and rightful Countess! And so our Little Bernie should've always been and was always meant to be! Long live the true and rightful Countess de Montfort! Hip, hip, hurray!"

"I've prayed for this event since the first day I pushed you on the swing, my Little Bernie!" revealed her former governess, Jeanne.

"I've wished for this day since Sweetheart first asked if she could help me turn the sheets and fluff up the pillows!" added chambermaid Félicitée.

"I've prayed for this moment since our Little Bernie first asked if she could stir the pot for me!" confided Andrée, the cook and leader of domestic staff.

Even those servants who come into family employ more recently voiced similar words of solid personal affection.

"I'm immensely touched by your long love and loyalty, Jeanne, Félicitée, Andrée, Pierrette, Therese, Yolande," their Little Bernie answered. She was providing each of her loyal followers, in turn, an equal heartfelt, grateful smile on her own red-painted lips. "Little Bernie will try never to disappoint you!"

"We know our Little Bernie won't disappoint!" the staff promised in joyous, enthusiastic unison. "Our Little Bernie is our mistress, our true mistress! She's always been our mistress! Long live the true and rightful Countess de Montfort-Alencon! Hurray! Hurray! Bravo! Bravo!"

"Hurray! Hurray!" enjoined all the others, ecstatic. Bravo! Bravo!"

"Now remove the child from the premises as quickly as you possibly can," instructed the dainty usurper, pointing to her twelve-year-old niece.

Still groggy, still weak, supine on a deep, comfortable, white couch, the now-deposed Celine just vaguely comprehended what was going on.

She barely understood a critical event in her life was transpiring.

"Even with all the crowds and traffic, my relatives should still be back by dinnertime," warned Madame de Charente, tying back her long dark brown hair. "So even with the extra time we've unexpectedly been provided, we must not delay."

"So true, Countess Bernie!" agreed with her devoted team.

"Before the rest of the family arrives back—and they eventually *will* arrive back," advised Madame de Charente, "your Countess Bernie needs to be fully, formally, and visibly installed in power! We must be able to confront the rest of the family with a *fait accompli.*–There must be no doubt at all in my relatives' and guests' mind as to who and who alone is now in control! Who and who alone everyone else now has no choice but to obey in all matters concerning the future and best interests of the House of Montfort!–There must be no question as to who henceforth wears the tiara! Your Little Bernie must have no one in a position to challenge her authority! Let us not merely be in charge but also—*look in charge*!!"

"The child," repeated Madame de Charente, indicating Celine, "must be removed from the premises as quickly as we possibly can! No one besides us must be able to reach the child for at least forty-eight hours! No one besides us this side of Heaven must know where the child is!"

"Long live the true and rightful Countess de Montfort!" cried the co-conspirators. "Hip, hip, hurray!"

"What about the two other children, Little Bernie?" inquired Pierrette, referring to Philippine and Leonie, who was attending the funeral. "What about the two other children?"

"No fear! That's being seen to," assured Madame de Charente. "The two other children are being escorted back from the funeral by Heloise and Martine in the limousine driven by Muhammad. Heloise, Martine, and Muhammad are loyal to your Countess, too. Instead of returning here, Muhammad will take the other children to a different location no one else in the family knows. The other children cannot be allowed to be used to challenge your Little Bernie's position as the new leader of the family and sole-director of all its current undertakings and future policies."

"We are," she freely confessed, still speaking in the collective plural, "as much a privately-owned firm, a targeted business enterprise, a political party as we are a—family. I'm afraid, poor Manon, now among the saints and angles, grossly forgot her worldly obligations."

"Countess Manon was meant for another calling in life, and the sweet, idealistic Dear," commented Jeanne.

So indeed Countess Manon was," agreed Félicitée. "She was meant for something other than the tiara."

"So sad," interjected Pierrette. "But we must not speak ill of the dead, especially of our Little Bernie's so sweet, gentle, tender sister."

All observed a moment of silence and made the sign of the cross.

"We were sure to get the younger children too," said Auntie Bernarde, she returning to current matters. "Philippine and Leonie are being sent to our estate in Brittany."

"Our Little Bernie, *my* Little Bernie thinks of everything!" remarked Jeanne in fond maternal praise.

"Ah! If only she'd been born a boy!" whispered Therese to Yolande, musing. "If she'd been born to wear trousers, she'd be another General de Gaulle!"

"Our Little Bernie is General de Gaulle in a skirt!" declared Yolande.

"Quite so!" agreed Therese. "Our Little Bernie is General de Gaulle in a skirt!"

Madame de Charente checked her delicate watch on the delicate wrist.

Next, she again pointed to her niece lying stupefied on the couch. "The child must also be out of Paris before nightfall. Paul, who flies our helicopter, supports us as well. It was Paul who enabled the alpiners to locate and recover Countess Manon's body. Her villa on Mt. Anne is halfway up the peak and only accessible by helicopter. Once I've got the child at Mt. Anne, only I can decide when she leaves. I will pay you all double—no—*triple* if you get the child to Mt. Anne before tomorrow night!"

"I'll pay each of you double—no—*triple* overtime," she promised, "if we succeed!"

"It will be done at once, our Little Bernie!" Auntie's supporters assured their mascot. "We guarantee to get the child to Mt. Anne before tomorrow night."

Powerfully-built Andrée—the cook and leader of domestic staff, exhibited a more assertive character, more physical energy, bigger muscles than most men. *The Stronger Sex l*ong ago learned the hard way not to contend with this particular weak female. Coming to the couch, she snatched up Celine and threw her over her left shoulder as if the child were a sack of potatoes or cattle feed. The twelve-year-old's groggy head now faced toward *the Persian Carpe*t floor.

"Ouch!" the woozy youngster mumbled. "Ooh!"

"Forgive me if I've hurt you, Cherie! I didn't mean to!" begged Andrée maternally to the sack of potatoes, animal feed slung over her left shoulder. "I love you honey—we all of us here love you so much– just as we still love your soft, kind Bob Dylan-fan Mama. We all of us here mean you well! One day, you'll understand what it all means– understand that we know what's best for you–One day, you'll thank us. Promise!"

Celine was too bewildered to reply.

"You're a real Sweet, Tender Precious! Just as Countess Manon was a real Sweet, Tender Precious," continued Andrée transporting the sack of potatoes, animal feed, head still toward the floor, into a dark wood foyer. "But this Dear is not a time or place. for a child!"

70

*S*weet, Tender Precious only mumbled.

"*There, there*, child!" comforted Andrée in a warm voice, she providing her sack of potatoes, animal feed, a loving, shielding pat on the bottom. "*There, there*, child! No need to worry your little brain about these complicated adult affairs. It will be a very long time before you ever need to tire yourself over dreary grownup matters."

At the front door, Celine, still tired and confused, was released to the ground. Her long, thick cherry blond hair covered her dazed twelve-year-old face. It was a twelve-year-old face frightened but not quite sure what to be frightened *about*.

Yolande and Pierrette, now taking charge, swiftly hustled Celine into a waiting stretch limousine. Afterward, they climbed in too, shut the door behind them, and with chauffeur Paul at the wheel, sped off.

"The child's been removed from the premises now, Countess Bernie–the child's gone," Therese called to those inside the house after she saw the vehicle disappear out the walled-off property's heavy, front, wrought-iron gate.. "The child's gone!"

"Where are Marie and Sabine?" asked Auntie Bernarde, she still in the Louis *XV Style*-salon, checking right and left. "Where are Marie and Sabine?"

"Here we are, Countess Bernie! Here we are!" the two teenage domestics announced, scurrying in, each carrying a heavy wooden, antique jewel box with both earnest girl's hands.

"Excellent! Do you have all the precious stones?" "Yes, we do, Countess Bernie." Good, good!"

Everyone collected back inside the salon.

"Let us be the ones in charge of you from now on!" supporters gleefully insisted to their: baby, little sister, chum, friend, heroin, inspiration, mascot, favorite doll. "Let us be in charge of you now, our Little Bernie!"

"If you wish it so, my dearest, most loyal, loving friends," replied Madame de Charente, providing each follower, in turn, a gracious, affectionate, vulnerable, ever-so feminine smile and twinkle of ladylike eyes. Careful too, she makes every glance unique to the eyes receiving her personal acknowledgment.

"So we wish!" called her followers, again in enthusiastic unison. "Then take me as you will! I'm not the Countess, and I'm *your* Countess!"

Madame de Charente was carried first to a red damask armchair with a brilliantly colored medieval tapestry hanging from the wall behind.

"No! I've got an even better idea for my splendid tiny, darling's grandest day!" said her former nanny, Jeanne.

"Excellent idea!" endorsed Félicitée, who once received Little Bernie's daily help turning the sheets and fluffing up the pillows. "As Little Bernie says, we must do all we can to make a strong appearance—demonstrate who's now unquestionably in command, who's the one and only legitimate leader of the House of Montfort-Alencon!"

"Let's all go to the dining hall!" instructed Jeanne.

Scurry

Patter

Skip

Scamper

Additional swift, dedicated, light feminine steps sounded down the corridor.

"Ouch! Ooh!"

Sorry, Little Bernie! We didn't mean to hurt you, Dear!"

Now it was Auntie Bernarde's turn to be Andrée's sack of potatoes, animal feed.

"Set the chair in front of the Georges de la Tour panorama!" Jeanne instructed the other domestic staff. Jeanne was the voice of an artist conscious she being in the process of creating a timeless masterpiece. "Right by the Prince d'Enghien–right by the *Grand Condé*–on his rearing white stallion! This will be perfect—and so historical, too—precisely what my baby girl has always deserved."

Madame de Charente was deposited in a cherry wood damask armchair set directly beneath the center of the huge dining room panorama. This demonstration of historical continuity, a show of unbroken march of political legitimacy, endorsement of the new by all ages passed, was apparent.

"Get the jewels!" ordered Jeanne feverishly. "I want to dress my baby girl!"

"The jewels!" cried Yolande, Therese, and Muhammad, each equally excited.

Madame de Charente pressed Jeanne's hand just as a child often pressed that of her cherished governess.

Baby Girl sat back, and she closed eyes, let a far wiser, greater, nobler person love and nurture her. First, Bernarde felt Jeanne place upon her surrogate daughter's body the *Carolingian* crucifix. Then, the strings of *Hapsburg* natural pearls and *Romanov, Safavid* emerald earrings; next, the *Capetian* topaz finger clasps and *Hohenstaufen* rubies. On her left wrist, Bernarde now wore the golden, jeweled *Byzantine* bracelet given by Justinian to Theodora.

On her right wrist, the stunning *Ottoman* bracelet was bestowed to Roxalina by Suleiman the Magnificent. Finally, atop Bernarde's mounds of long, thick brown hair was placed the tiara of red, blue, and green *Gupta Period* diamonds.

When the servant's mascot, at last, reopened her eyes, Jeanne, Félicitée, Andrée, Pierrette, and all the others were on their knees. Either merrily cooing or happily weeping as they surveyed their grandest creation.

"Long live the true and rightful Countess de Montfort-Alencon!" all cried, rising as one to feet. "Long live our Countess Bernie!"

ALLEGRO

"HOW DID I DO IT that time? Did I finally perform it correctly, Auntie Bernarde?" pleaded her eldest niece after completing another ungainly attempt. "Sorry, sorry! I mean *Countess de Montfort*! I'm trying all I can to follow all your precise instructions."

"No! No, you imbecile! Could you do it again, Celine? I told you to do it in the *other* direction, the *left*!"

The youngster made an additional earnest but flawed attempt.

"*There*. Did I do it properly at last, Countess de Montfort? I'm trying all I can to get it for you."

"No, still no!" reprimanded Auntie Bernarde.

Celine cringed with fear as the dainty drill sergeant stamped her left foot, glared with furious refined disapproval up-close, directly into her pretty adolescent ward's meek face. A long bamboo stick in the teacher's right hand, she tapped it on the waxed hardwood ballroom floor in a threatening manner.

SMACK

"Imbecile! How could poor, dear Manon have ever possibly created you! Maybe the nurses at the maternity hospital got the babies mixed up! You're just an imbecile! Everyone has a cross to bear, and apparently you, *Mademoiselle Feather-brains*, are my appointed burden!"

SMACK

From the wall to the left hung a painting by Degas similarly portraying a male dancing teacher lording over a young student.

"I'm sorry, Countess. I don't want to be just across you've got to bear. I don't want to be just a *Mademoiselle Feather-brains!*"

"No, no, I can see you really don't, Child," conceded Auntie Bernard. "Anyway, how would it reflect on me if I was never able to make you follow my instructions? Now watch me. It's simple if you do it all in one single, uninterrupted motion. Then, it should be no trouble. Now, watch me."

She demonstrated the motion with incomparable grace. Then, I demonstrated it a second time with no less incomparable grace.

"See, Child! It's simple! Simple!"

Yet a third time, the teacher performed the motion with matchless style.

"But I'm only a girl, Countess," begged her niece. "It's difficult for me to remember. I'm only a girl."

SMACK

SMACK

SMACK—of stick-on plodding child's little fanny.

Celine burst into tears, hid her face in trembling hands, sobbed.

Her socks drooped.

"Foolishness, foolishness!" shouted Madame de Charente, deeply annoyed with her student's continued lackluster performance. "I, too, was once *only a girl*. Yet I had no trouble learning! Your noble, departed Mama, she now with all the saints and angels, was once *only a girl*, and she had no problem learning! Elizabeth, I was once *only a girl*! Eleanor of Aquitaine was once *only a girl*!

She was soon reminding: "Simone Weil, Marie Curie, Jeanne d'Arc, Catherine the Great, St. Teresa of Avila, Mrs. Roosevelt, St. Hildegard of Bingen, Georgia O'Keeffe, Edith Wharton, St. Catherine of Siena, George Eliot, Blanche of Castile, Jane Austen, Boadicea, Ada Lovelace, Sister Juana Ines de la Cruz, Emily Dickinson, Anna Akhmatova, Charlotte, and Emily Bronte, Virginia Woolf, Berthe Morisot, Marie Laurencin, Anna Pavlova, Marina Tsvetaeva, Anne Frank, Sarah Bernhardt, Sigrid Undset, Mrs. Thatcher, Angela Merkel were all, each, too once *only a girl*!"

SMACK

"So, I'll hear no more of this stupid—*but I'm only a girl* foolishness!" admonished Auntie. "Do you hear me! Do you hear me!"

MACK

"Yes, Countess Bernarde," pleaded her niece, sniffling; eyes red; ashamed; cheek, stinging. "There will be no more of this—*I'm only a girl*—foolishness. I promise!"

"Good! Because you'll regret it if you ever even once dare break that promise! Now perform the physical move I instructed you, again!"

SMACK

After first pulling up her socks, Celine, at last, performed the required maneuver with incomparable grace.

"Magnificent! Perfect! I couldn't have done it better myself!" declared Madame de Charente, clapping avidly ladylike, next adjusting her short gray skirt. "Brilliant! I couldn't have done it better myself! You've got a splendid raw gift for it! You've got plenty of raw talent! But it requires training, discipline. Unfortunately, because that clear skill, aptitude was neglected for so long, my training of you must be doubly rigorous, severe. You've tremendous potential, Dear, and I, ought to know!"

Celine was too overcome with emotion to respond.

She could only make a good-little-girl grin of thanks.

Her socks drooped.

Madame de Charente smiled back at her young charge, regally. Her expression was monarchical in its degree of positive endorsement, royal, in its unqualified admiration. *"See.* I said all you needed is to perform it in one single, uninterrupted motion! Then, Dear, it's simple."

"Yes, Countess Bernarde, all I need is to perform it in one single, uninterrupted motion! Then it's simple."

Celine repeated the maneuver with the same matchless beauty and grace.

"Bravo! Bravo!" proclaimed Madame de Charente clapping avidly ladylike. "Since it's plainly so simple for you, Dear, show me a third time."

Celine made a third splendid performance.

"Bravo! Bravo! Soon I'll never get you to stop, Dear!" congratulated Madame de Charente, giving her niece a loving, tender, protective kiss on each cheek. "Bravo! Bravo! Soon I'll never get you to stop!"

"The Virgin bless, you! The Virgin bless, you, Countess Bernarde!" sobbed Celine immensely touched upon receiving her stern Mistress's gingerly-offered praise.

The youngster embraced her exacting guardian as if the stern adult were a precious religious object. Celine covered Madame de Charente's face and neck with passionately reverent kisses. She pressed her own needy face against the majestic lady's formidable but welcoming large bust. "Bless you, bless you so, so much, Countess Bernarde!"

"Maybe soon, Dear," said Madame de Charente, gently stroking her niece's long, thick, cherry blond hair, "you'll possess enough self-confidence to do the maneuver without me needing to smack you first!"

"Yes, Countess Bernarde" answered Celine sniffling, teary-eyed, she clutching her guardian no less needy. "Yes, Countess Bernarde. Maybe soon I'll possess enough self-confidence to perform the maneuver without you needing to smack me first."

"So you hope, will!"

Life wasn't easy for Celine.

It wasn't intended to be.

The days of freely-given privilege, of being petted and pampered, were over. No longer she guaranteed the tiara through mere accident of birth. Celine now needed first to show herself deserving to be accepted as a leader of the great clan. As in the case of confronting the horseman in the Georges De La Tour panorama, Philippine Luria and Léonie Golitsyn had no difficulty adapting to and then excelling in their new, more demanding environment. As previously, too, their elder sister, Celine, required more time.

Following twelve months during which she swift, expertly, restored the Montfort Ladies to all their traditional power and influence, Countess Bernarde announced that she might be prepared to serve only as family regent. Should her eldest niece attained full intellectual, emotional and physical maturity, the *Gupta Period* tiara would then pass into Celine's hands. If, and when, her eldest niece could again address her simply as Auntie Bernarde, remained, however, entirely the regent's personal decision.

While romantic, noble-heart Countess Manon went into the family business reluctantly and only because she was permitted no alternative, her less idealistic but more practical younger sister, also given no alternative, made a virtue of necessity. In so doing, Madame de Charente became the finest grand courtesan of her generation. She illustrated how a prisoner, if adept, can use her gilded cage to subtly dominate both her jailers and the very culture keeping her forever confined.

That uneducated but artistic or intellectually gifted teenage girls from throughout Europe facing the same future as Madame de Charente at their age eagerly sought apprenticeship under her in Paris was no surprise. The grand courtesan was universally acknowledged not just as the best at her particular craft but indisputably, its finest teacher. She also provided her young charges free room and board, free meals, clothing, and health services. But most important for any ambitious little newcomer, Madame de Charente's endorsement provided access to the otherwise impenetrable social world of the wealthy, influential, still politically powerful French landed elite and titled aristocracy. Perhaps, thanks to their great teacher's help, the day might come when these poor, unloved, unwanted, sometimes physically-abused daughters were each to be remembered in history as another Diane of Poitiers, Gabrielle d'Estrées, Madame. de Pompadour, or Madame de Stael!

The odds of any individual youngster from the provinces or farther afield being selected were wider than for she obtaining an invitation to have tea along with the Queen of England. There were so many requests for so few openings. Just a handful of each year's army of girls seeking entrance to the *Baroque* townhouse (every one of them undoubtedly talented) could ever hope to pass the rigorous (no second try) examination and personal interview. All the same, a particularly gifted few were indeed able to beat the odds.

For years without fail, every Sunday morning and twice daily on all major religious holidays, Madame de Charente was observed passing through the historic, enclosed garden running parallel the Right embankment on her way to Mass. Apprentices scurried devotedly after her two-by-two as a uniform flock of meek, gentle *Little Dears* obedient to Mistress's every command. Were Madame de Charente a nun, the sight would appear an adolescent version of a *Madeline* story.

That the kids' distinguished guardian was fully entitled to expect and receive such devoted loyalty was made abundantly clear to each girl on the day of her first arrival. When overtime some novice inevitably forgot the rules or was unwise enough to raise a challenge, the little miscreant in short order learned the painful consequences on her rear end. The rest of the flock, on such occasions solemnly summoned to witness and meditate upon the fate of "troublemakers," "silly-heads," "bad girls," never needed reminding what was expected of them.

"This is a training institution," explained the prioress sternly, "not a democracy!"

Yet In another sense, cream color, Baroque No. 3 Rue Artemis was also a family and Madame de Charente, the mother.

"However, it's not one of those: *Sixties,* Dr. Spock, being-*fulfilled,* grading-on-the-curve, call-your-parent-by-first-name, no spankings, *New Math* kind of families–mind you, my little misses!" swift Auntie Bernarde amended lest her young listeners develop unwarranted ideas. "No! This isn't Greenwich Village or California! No girls are permitted wearing trousers, cutting their hair short, or smoking marijuana, here! Mother is going to be your *mother*, not your friend! This isn't that kind of American *do-your-own-thing* family where the children receive so much *understanding* and *sympathy* that the pampered brats end up later either: never leaving home, dropping out of university, having five divorces, becoming drug addicts. Or, they were spending enough money rambling on to analysts about their sexual frustration as to purchase a yacht! Far from it! This is a proper family!"

"A proper family" Madame de Charente illuminated, "which, through fostering personal discipline, through honoring legitimately held authority, by encouraging and doing all to promote real talent, amply rewarding work truly well done while not excusing slackers and ignoramuses, enables its progeny to provide a noble, useful contribution to the world!

"Therefore," summarized Madame de Charente, "as long as you little misses live under my roof, are my personal responsibility *in loco parentis*, I possess the rightful authority, and moral obligation to teach and care for you as I know is in my children's long-term best interests! And in the grand scheme of things, the mother *does* know best! That philandering gangster Bonaparte should have listened to his Mama when she warned him not to invade Russia! But oh, no. Bonaparte thought he knew better than the one who bore him. As we all know, even Bonaparte soon acknowledged that Mama *does* know best!"

Those "little misses" considering the house rules overly severe today, she prophesied confidently, would later insist their own gifted "little misses" be raised in a similar vigorous fashion.

Contrary to what Twenty-first Century progressive social theorists and educators might expect, the uniform flock of *Little Misses* dutifully scurrying for decades after Madame de Charente as if in a Madeline story, did so neither out of fear, reluctance, nor submissiveness. Quite the opposite!

To most of the teenagers under her strict supervision, Madame de Charente was the first strong, assertive, self-confident female personality they ever met. For some girls, a mere first encounter with their stern but the inspiring teacher was a positive life-changing event. Madame de Charente was someone who sincerely deserved the unfortunately all too over-used and diluted title of *Role Model*.

Each apprentice was desperate to obtain her guardian's distant, monarchical, never unqualified, but always genuine personal approval. The harder that lofty queen's favor became to receive, the harder her subjects instinctively worked to win it. If remaining in the empress's good graces might be swiftly lost again should its lucky possessor grow lazy, that girl understood she must never slack at her studies or permit her new high quality of work decline. *No pain, no gain, no guts, no glory.*

For some kids, their demanding, exacting, never totally satisfied judge was a surrogate parent—the special individual every child above all wishes to make rightly proud. For her devoted flock, their loving disciplinarian was Truth, Goodness, Beauty incarnate. Her voice, the font of all wisdom.

From one perspective, Madame de Charente was equivalent to an abbess of a famous, historic convent. From another angle, she was comparable to an inspiring leader on the battlefield. She and her loyal novices or crack-infantry regiment were dedicated either to the contemplation of a lofty ideal or the defense of a great cause.

The girls frequently requisitioned Madame de Charente in the hall, dining room, or the townhouse's garden so they might kiss and hug her, caress her long brown hair. Pretending at first to put up a struggle, Madame de Charente quickly surrendered to her adorers' will. The mailbox was often jammed with letters and sets of photographs from former students, both chronicling their own successful activities since graduation and insisting their teacher made it all possible. A few of the writers even addressed Madame de Charente as *Mama.*

None scurried after her Mistress with more devotion, tried harder to win, and was at last rewarded with her teacher's never freely-given approval, none clutched her guardian's body tighter, adopted more phrases of her elder's speech, or fondled her patroness's hair more lovingly than Celine.

Lest, Madame de Charente ever be accused of nepotism or of unfairly relaxing the entrance examination and house rules of conduct for a late, beloved sister's daughter, she was deliberately extra-demanding on Celine's test for admittance. And after the girl passed anyway, her teacher was even stricter than usual with the new student's training. Only twice did Madame de Charente exhibit preference. First: when she was insisting Celine delay a year before taking the tough school examination; second: when ten years later, Madame de Charente fulfilled her promise to eventually hand over the red, blue, green Gupta Period diamond tiara.

During the intervening decade, however, no apprentice so often frustrated her Mistress through exhibiting poor behavior or received more spankings, smacks, denials of dinner, was given more significant numbers of banishment to the bedroom, temporary loss of visiting-rights, reprimands for inadequate work, insufficient study, inattention to valuable detail, than–Celine. Madame de Charente made meticulously certain nothing whatsoever could divert this particularly troublesome charge from at last achieving her whole, long overlooked, neglected ability. That ability being–Celine's skill to ultimately prove herself even greater than her historic, celebrated teacher.

Idle musings, fond daydreams now ended. This afternoon's adult Celine reverently set each beautiful lady in a gilt-framed studio photograph side by side above the same marble top *Queen Anne*-walnut chest of drawers.

"From this moment forth," she told them, "I'm keeping your two pictures together! Mama, you put some big, beautiful, noble, priceless ideas and theories into my simple head. And Auntie Bernarde, you enabled me to make sure Mama's gifts became more than just ideas and theories!"

ETUDE ON A PREVIOUS THEME

"THOSE NEW SNAPSHOTS OF THE garden are first-rate, Mama! They're positively awesome!" warmly endorsed miniature Ferdinande de Godefroy, who just arrived in the banquet hall. Unlike five-foot-six-inches in stocking feet Rolande de Montfort, her half-sister was only four feet ten. This shorter, if senior sibling by two years wore a strapless, silk ball gown colored lapis-lazuli. Precious Japanese natural pearls and stunning *Romanov* diamonds decorated the pint-sized girl's lovely bare shoulders, sculpted neck, and ears. Like her mother, she had long cherry-blond hair. When allowed running free, these thick locks descended like her parents to a narrow waist. Presently, Celine's elder daughter chose to tie her main back for the ten-thousand-euros-a-plate dinner she was attending tonight at the *World Bank* with its President, her lover, the Duc d'Aveyron.

"Yes, those new snapshots of the garden are first-rate, Mama! They are positively awesome!" reiterated Ferdinande de Godefroy. "They are great, marvelous! You are a real photographer, Mama! One of the best around these days! No doubt about it! And I'm not merely speaking my usual *Female Foolishness* or *Witless Woman* jabber! Why even flibbertigibbets like me can tell, Mama was born with a special gift! One, which shouldn't be either ignored or abandoned! I'm going to tell His Grace the Duc d'Aveyron all about it! I won't stop nagging, pestering His Grace until he agrees to come to see the pictures, too!"

"I'll also make sure," she promised," that His Grace then tells everybody who is *anybody* in financial circles that my Mama is an artist if there ever was an artist!"

"Thank you so much, Chere Petite," responded Countess de Montfort humbly, she giving a grateful, protective kiss to her child's no less pretty face. "I'm so pleased you enjoy the photos. Just tell His Grace that your Mama is trying to do the best a feeble woman can."

"Well, I'm personally going to make sure everybody who is *anybody* here in Paris soon knows about your 'feeble' gift!" guaranteed Ferdinande de Godefroy, pressing her parent's hands tight to illustrate daughter's boundless conviction. "The world must know my Mama is a great artist!"

The enthusiastic newcomer turned to leave.

"Wait, tiny dear!" summoned Celine. "I must first make sure you look perfect for this evening's grand ceremony. Remember, Chere Petite, and tonight will be the first official event at which His Grace the Duc d'Aveyron appears since the so unfortunate, so unexpected death of Her Grace the Duchesse Louise. On this occasion, her widower will especially need his intimate, pocket-size friend beside him. His Grace the Duke will especially require you, his loyal confidante, to provide him selfless, unwavering, nourishing, feminine support. Sometimes, even those all-mighty people who wear trousers require a weak creature in a skirt to lean upon! That's why Mama wants her favorite Little Mouse to be a child's prettiest."

"The six-month period of official mourning ended yesterday," Celine reminded, brushing her elder daughter's own long, thick cherry blond hair. "A very important personal and family issue you and His Grace recognized was quite inappropriate, ill-mannered, unchristian to mention earlier, can now henceforth be legitimately discussed. It can, at last, be tastefully settled. Life does move on! I learned that myself when my own Mama died. We aren't morbid Victorians. Also, no one with an ounce of sense was previously ignorant of the relationship between you two. The issue needs to finally be settled once and for all, not kept dangling. It needs to be given the sanction of the Church."

"I'm sure," she added, "that even poor late Duchesse Louise, now with all the saints and angels in Heaven, would agree."

Celine motioned Ferdinande de Godefroy to halt.

"Now stand-still, Chere Petite. Mama wants you to appear your best!"

The grand courtesan fiddled with the apprentice's jewelry and hairpins.

Next, she applied progeny's new lipstick and mascara.

Then, pulled her daughter's revealing gown.

Emphasizing yet more the teenager's firm, welcoming, unblemished body.

"What my gentle Ferdinande at first appears to lack in brains or personal ambition, she certainly makes up for in more traditional feminine qualities," judged her mother, admiring offspring's pretty face, smooth rosy skin, graceful figure, wide cleavage. "Besides, in her new social position, this kind, simple *Thing* is far better off not initially appearing to have any brains or personal ambition! Brains, personal ambition, when too visible in a woman, always frightens men. They only make a woman's road to success more difficult, her life unhappy."

"For someone your size, you've certainly got a splendid bust, Chere Petite. A bust, as fine, impressive as a girl twice your size! God bestows our sex gifts with the clear intention those gifts be used, taken advantage of, be employed for constructive purposes. Why else would Our Father provide them! It's sinful to challenge the wishes of Our Father."

"Yes, Mama, so it is!" dutifully replied Ferdinande de Godefroy, less than five feet tall. "We must never challenge the wishes of Our Father."

"Or those of our *Mother*?"

"No, no! I would never even think to challenge your wishes, Mama! I've long understood you know what's best. It's only proper for Mama to make the decisions, only proper for Mama to give the instructions! All I hope is that when carrying out your decisions when following your instructions, I can make Mama proud of me."

"Fear not, my darling. You will always make your Mama immensely proud!"

Celine rewarded her daughter with a peck on the cheek, affectionate pat to fanny.

"From your birth, Mama has raised you to be a faithful Christian?"

"Yes, Mama. I've always been a faithful Christian, thanks to you."

"Mama taught you to daily twice recite the *Rosary,* to retain a special place in your heart for Our Lady, The Virgin?"

"Yes, Mama. I recite the *Rosary* twice every day. I keep a really special place in my heart for Our Lady, The Virgin."

"Excellent! So nice! Just as it should be! Mama also raised you to attend Mass weekly without fail and twice on all major religious holidays. She taught you to go monthly to Confession?"

"Yes, Mama. I go to Mass every week without fail, twice on all major religious holidays. I go monthly to Confession."

"Become a member of the Altar Guild?"

"Yes, Mama, I'm a member of the Altar Guild." "You give a tithe of your income to worthy causes?"

"Yes Mama" assured Ferdinande de Godefroy. "I give a tithe of my income to worthy causes."

"Well then," concluded Celine, stepping two paces back so she might fondly survey her completed makeup and sartorial work. "As my Auntie Bernarde–your *Great* Auntie Bernarde–advised me long ago, ‹helping others doesn't mean we can't also help *ourselves.*' The only way we will be able always to help others is by first securing ourselves in a position from which we can always provide that help!"

"Yes, Mama," promised Ferdinande de Godefroy, she took the hint. Girl's knowing smile indicating Mother's china doll possessed infinitely more brains and ambition than all but a handful realized. "Yes, Mama, I will make sure the issue is settled with His Grace tonight and before we even go to bed!"

"Ooh! Just think of it! My Chere Petite is to become a duchess!" cooed, giggled Celine. "Ooh! Mama will need to curtsey to her, now! Mama will need to address Chere Petite as 'Your Grace!' After all, I'm only a humdrum countess."

Parent curtseyed to child, deep.

"Please don't do that, Mama!" begged Ferdinande de Godefroy, embarrassed. "Being curtseyed to by my Mama–she addressing me as 'Your Grace'–is unfair and wrong! Most of all, it's–*silly*! The Countess de Montfort, who is directly descended from Charlemagne and Otto the Great, is the one who is owed a show of deference and respect from all the kings and queens of Europe!"

Ferdinande de Godefroy curtseyed to Mama, deep.

Two true-blonds acknowledged one another in like motion. "Mama?"

"Yes, Chere Petite?"

"Would you also like to come over to the palace for lunch tomorrow? Perhaps you'll be present when the personal issue between me and His Grace the Duc d'Aveyron is formally, legally, concluded to our mutual satisfaction?"

"Oh, I'd love to Chere Petite," answered Celine, "but tomorrow morning, I've also got something very important to do. I've got my own major issue to settle."

SO, WHO SHOULD COME NEXT?

MORE WAS ON COUNTESS DE Montfort's mind the following morning than simply obtaining a unanimous vote allocating funds to repair drought-damaged **Pascale Kedari Memorial Park**. Her present fifth consecutive two-year term as chairman of the *Ladies Garden Fund* was also set to expire in a few months. She knew she would have no trouble winning near-unanimous (9-1) election to yet a sixth go-round. No reason existed why she could not remain chairman for the rest of her refined, elegant life! Weighed-down with so many new and unanticipated extra civic responsibilities and social commitments, however, Countess de Montfort decided privately not to seek a sixth term. She had absolutely no intention leaving the board altogether, though. Or, of withdrawing her continued influence, mind you! Just relinquishing the chairmanship.

Stepping down after being chiefly responsible for both restoring the famous, historic flowerbeds and for guaranteeing the park's original loveliness into the indefinite future seemed an ideal moment was concluding a decade of critical leadership. For someone with the Countess's keen theatrical sensibilities, there could be no more melodramatic a point to depart the center stage.

Yet, who should be Celine's successor?

For most members of the *Ladies Garden Trust,* preservation of the flowerbeds was just a part-time interest. Not one to be taken casually, but still just a part-time interest. Participation on the governing board was, but one of the many suitably-feminine, unquestionably-ladylike, generally faith-based forms of volunteer work every wife, mistress, significant-other, mother, daughter or sister in this privileged social class had for centuries been required performing in the larger community.

"It's every woman's *Christian Duty*," explained agnostic Countess Manon to Celine, Philippine, and Leonie. "Even a woman who isn't a

Christian must still take part! It's the responsibility of women to set for the world a good example."

"After all," counseled deeply devout Auntie Bernarde, "if we women don't do our *Christian Duty,* who will! Certainly not those stupid, full-of-themselves men!"

We're sure you're always right, Celine, sweetheart!" regularly pledged Madame de Morbihan, Madame de Toledano, Madame de Lanceau, Madame de Rousillon, and the chairman's other faithful, longtime allies. With their own participation on the garden board frequently interrupted by the requirement to–supervise charity bazaars; promote flood and famine relief; to find homes for widows and orphans; to chair cultural, environmental, or missionary societies; arrange church dinners; teach poor girls Catechism; award agricultural prizes that their family established; teach children of their tenants to play piano–these other noble dames long permitted their chairman to make all the major decisions about the precious green space. "We're sure you're absolutely right, Celina Sweetheart," they always assured."If that's what you think is best for the garden, fine! We'll vote for it. No one knows more about flowerbeds than you, our energetic Celine."

None of these colleagues, their leader calculated, should be her successor. Even if they were each no less dedicated to preserving the exquisite flora, not one possessed enough free time to take up the responsibility with sufficient determination. "It isn't the chairman's role to simply follow a policy set by others," observed Countess de Montfort, revealing the near-unquestioned style of executive authority she wielded. "It's the role of the chairman to personally formulate that policy and then see to it others carry out her policy with all proper speed, skill, and commitment."

So, if not these four previously mentioned ladies, nor the equally worthy but often distracted Baroness de Rochambeau, Madame de Perrault, Madame de Beaumont, or Madame de Marly, then who?

Who was left to take up the reigns of command with all the commitment and determination the current chairman believed was essential in her successor?

"There's also Mrs. Robertson Villers!" observed Countess de Montfort, her long, thick, sinuous, cherry blond hair at last brushed to personal satisfaction. "If that Persian girl rarely agrees with me, she's also just as actively committed to protecting the park! Mrs. Villers appears on television speaking up for the park. She writes articles for the newspapers in support of the park. She's certainly got strong and fierce dedication–strong and fierce opinions as to how the park can be preserved from those idiots wearing trousers! No need I ever fear she'll lose interest or run out of enthusiasm—least of all should I fear she'll compromise on what she thinks is truly right! That Persian girl has got the makings of a leader!"

"I've got to speak to Mrs. Villers about this and in private," the countess pledged.

She was much taken with her new idea.

"I'll hand the chairmanship over to Mrs. Villers! I'll hand the chairmanship over to Mrs. Villers!"

A wide, hopeful, adolescent smile commanded Mme. de Montfort's newly red painted lips. A girlish twinkle in her green, ever-so feminine eyes further illustrated excitement.

Likely this decision had been quietly germinating in her subconscious for a long time. Yet when last voicing it, she felt as if receiving a revelation from on high.

"I so-so love you, Blessed Virgin!" exclaimed Celine, kissing the religious medallion around her slender neck. "What a marvelous, exciting day you've made it for me, Blessed Virgin!"

THE ENIGMA VARIATIONS

WHEN THE TWO DISTINGUISHED LADIES, at last, met an hour later in the first-floor salon of No. 3 Rue Artemis beneath a famous Manet, they were hardly chatterboxes. Never previously had these celebrated rivals been alone together. No friends or allies were present to give Celine and Ashraf encouragement or protection. No benevolent third party could be depended upon to either divert the conversation, offer pretext to leave the room, or shift responsibility for managing this critical event.

"Fine morning is it not, Mrs. Villers?"

"Yes. It is a fine morning, Countess de Montfort."

"That's a lovely outfit you're wearing, Mrs. Villers."

"And that's a lovely outfit *you're* wearing, too, Countess."

"It's splendid what you've done with your hair, Mrs. Villers."

"And it's splendid what you've done with *your* hair, Countess."

"You've got such a cute pair of heels, Mrs. Villers."

"And *you've* got such a cute pair, *too*, Countess."

"I hope it wasn't a terrible inconvenience you were coming early so we might speak privately and in confidence, Mrs. Villers," pleaded Celine as she and her guest having first meandered the *Queen Anne* dinner hall under portraits of *Montfort Ladies* painted by Reynolds, Copley, and West now stopped to survey the photos of their park's drought-stricken flowerbeds, vines, and trees.

"No, not at all, Countess. I'm an early-riser."

"So too, were both my dear mother Countess Marie," replied her daughter, pointing to a nude by Rothko, "and also my precious auntie Countess Bernarde," niece then gesturing to a nude by Andy Warhol.

"They each told me: '*Don't sleep your life away, Celine. You've only got so many days on earth, and those you let slip by witho*ut *making practical use of them, won't be coming back. You won't have a second chance.*'"

Some framed new images of the enclosed garden were placed above a polished walnut *Chippendale* luncheon table; others were set atop a burnished ebony secretary. Still, more new pictures of the vegetation rested atop a lustrous oak chest of drawers with shined brass shelf handles.

Celine wore: a short, pattern, sleeveless dress; neutral-shade pantyhose; white heels; a pearl necklace with a gold crucifix. Madame's long, thick, cherry blond hair was tied back. Her body conveyed a timeless, delicate, vulnerable fragrance.

Ashraf wore: a similar short, pattern, sleeveless dress; neutral-shade pantyhose; red heels; a pearl necklace without a gold crucifix. Her long, thick black hair was tied back. Her body, too, conveyed a timeless, delicate, vulnerable fragrance.

"I'm sure you certainly didn't expect receiving a request to come and speak with me in private and in confidence, Mrs. Villers! But life has its surprising turns. And well, it should! That's my personal view! Life would be terribly dull if there were no surprises, no unexpected events!"

"So indeed, Countess," replied the newcomer, polite but suspicious.

"Is Messalina attempting to maneuver me into some trap?" pondered Ashraf. Considering the pair's long fractious relationship, this supposition was not at all paranoid. "Is Messalina about to ask me to– *resign for the larger good of the trust?*"

Uncomfortable silent moments atop adjoining damask chairs elapsed.

Each lady crossed her pretty legs, opposite.

Hem of own short dress receding.

A further painting on the wall, this time one by Gericault, depicted yet another earlier Montfort Lady. Reclining nude aboard a sumptuous raft as Cleopatra, she glided languorous down the Nile accompanied by her devoted, Mark Antony-clad Lord Byron.

"You're a United States citizen, is that not correct, Mrs. Villers?" interjected the Montfort clan's current leader cheerily.

"Yes, I am Countess. So are my parents and my sister. My older sister Golbihar represented the Unite States three consecutive times at the Winter Olympics."

"How wonderful, Mrs. Villers! You must be so proud!"

"Yes, I am, Countess. On each of the three occasions, Golbihar won a gold medal at Ladies Figure Skating. That's never been equaled. It also likely never will."

"Most impressive, Mrs. Villers!"

Wishing to impress her *Educated* guest with facts the *Uneducated* hostess acquired in recent weeks while she was perusing Rolande's large book and academic journal collection, Celine observed: "Were you aware Mrs. Villers that General Eisenhower was not originally the one appointed by Roosevelt to command Operation Overlord? The original commander—his name suddenly slips my Scatterbrained little head– was killed in a plane crash on his way to Washington DC, and so General Eisenhower was selected in his place."

"If that hadn't happened," she laughed, "later-on, instead of—*I like Ike*—people might have been saying—*Go with Joe, Bob for the Job*—or something of that nature."

"Indeed, Countess."

"I much admire General Eisenhower. I think he should be acknowledged as a great man. What is your opinion, Mrs. Villers?"

"If he hadn't sent the *CIA* to overthrow democratically-elected Muhammad Mossaddegh and restore the absolutist Shah, the situation in Persia today would be much different."

"All the same, General Eisenhower experienced a surprising turn in his life."

"And so too did the officer whose plane crashed, Countess!"

"I've long been fascinated by history, Mrs. Villers. My younger daughter, Rolande, is too. Of course, *Missy* is far more adept at the subject than her *Scatterbrained* Mama. My little *Missy* is what you Americans call a *Whiz*. You should see *Missy*'s library upstairs! The child's so smart, learned, and insightful on all sorts of learned subjects! Mama tries her feeble best to keep up."

"My own area is mathematics, Countess."

"Ooh! Mathematics! I am ever so impressed, Mrs. Villers! They say—whoever these omnipotent *they* are—that girls aren't good at mathematics. Of course, I've learned through life experience that if a girl says—'Bugger *they*'—sorry for my unladylike language Mrs. Villers—a girl can accomplish many things *they* claim she's not supposed to be up to. Take Marie Curie, for instance."

"I fully agree, Countess."

"Or, like my little Rolande's heroine, Simone Weil."

"Like my own heroine, Eleanor of Aquitaine!"

Several additional mutually uncomfortable silent moments passed.

Celine emitted a dainty forced cough, fiddled with her hair.

Ashraf emitted a dainty forced cough, fiddled with her hair.

Each lady checked her *Hermes Birkin* handbag.

Crossed own pretty legs, opposite

Hem of short dress receding.

"Do you have any children, Mrs. Villers?"

"I had a daughter, but she died very young."

"Oh, I'm so terribly, terribly sorry, Mrs. Villers!" pleaded Celine earnestly, fearful she just raised a painful, taboo subject. "Please, please, please forgive me! I hope my gauche, rude, intrusive words didn't upset you too much?"

"No, no Countess. Rebecca died some years ago, and I've been reconciled to it."

"Well, be rest assured, never doubt, Mrs. Villers, that your little Rebecca is now with The Virgin in Heaven."

"Bless you, Countess! That's so sweet of you to show such concern!"

Each lady fiddled with her necklace.

Spied her *Cartier* watch.

Crossed her own pretty legs, opposite.

Hem of short dress receding.

Not since she has been resigned to receiving Auntie Bernarde's frequent smacks and scoldings did Celine feel less in command of the situation. If she never before in such intimate contact with mathematician Ashraf Kermanshani, that same individual's mere physical presence manifested in some mysterious, indefinable manner the embodiment of a truly superior mind and soul. For the spectator, this experience was as frightening as stimulating.

A cold, fearful shiver raced Celine's spine.

Her heart took an extra, unnerving beat.

She sensed again, being just twelve years old, her knee socks drooping, flat shoes unbuckled, her braids come undone.

Celine felt dreadfully stupid, petty, insignificant. She now something– *but come with the dust and gone with the wind.*

"This must be just what people experienced when they first confronted Bonaparte," postulated Celine under her breath. Ardent monarchists, the *Montfort Ladies* even today still refuse to call 'that upstart, full-of-himself, Corsican gangster' **Napoleon.** "People got weak in the knees, got lightheaded, sick in the tummy when first meeting Bonaparte. They became confused, felt stupid, frightened. No wonder that scoundrel usually got from them exactly what he was after!"

She is soon adding: "If someone ever needs to be tossed off a lifeboat so it won't sink, it'll be me going overboard, *not* Mrs. Villers! 'We're dreadfully sorry, Celine sweetheart,' they'll tell me, 'but you must go to the sharks so we can save brilliant Mrs. Villers. Now be a good little girl and don't make any trouble– off-you-go.' Splash, gobble-gobble.'"

Nevertheless, this same unnerving sense of being in the presence of someone truly extraordinary, which confirmed to Celine she was correct in her choice of successor.

"Those are very beautiful photographs, Countess" said Ashraf, both sincerely admiring the pictures and unaware others might find her presence so intimidating. "You're an artist! That term—*artist*—is bandied about so frequently these days it's been hideously diluted. But you, Countess, you are an *artist* in the original and true definition of the word! You might also consider having the pictures published. Truly! I'm not kidding! I'm sure many people with interest in photography will buy copies. Perhaps the book can also be used to raise additional funds for the garden."

"That's ever so kind of you to say so, Mrs. Villers. I'm flattered—I took these photos specifically for the luncheon—However, I've actually been a camera enthusiast for a number of years now. Just listen to my elder daughter, Ferdinande! Perhaps one day, when you've got the free time, I could show you some of my other photographs?"

"Yes, but of course you may, Countess."

"I'll also seriously consider your advice to publish the photographs, Mrs. Villers."

"Excellent, excellent, Countess! Others must see your fine work." Celine paused.

Crossed her pretty legs, opposite.

Hem of short dress receding.

"You're *educated*, Mrs. Villers. Where I come from, girls don't go to school. Perhaps—you might possibly consider–writing a preface for my little photography book?—I'm sure an intellectual like you is the exact person needed to write it—You'll know how to make my little book appeal to—attract the interest of—other *educated* people–win the interest of people who come from places were girls do go to school."

"I'd be honored, Countess. I'll be delighted to assist if that's what you really want. Although speaking from personal experience, let me assure you a great many of those 'educated,' 'intellectual' people you refer to, are not really as 'educated' or as 'intellectual' as you think!"

The two genteel ladies again meandered the spacious *Queen Anne* style banquet hall decorated with ancestral Montfort portraits by Hals and Ruysdael. As they did so, however, each dame clearly detected the aloof, distant, suspicious atmosphere of just minutes earlier rapidly give way to an environment both women found relaxed, intimate, even comradely.

"Now, why exactly did you wish peaking in private this morning, Countess?"

"It's because I've got an important favor to ask of you, Mrs. Villers."

"You're asking a favor of *me,* Countess? I'm sure you don't need my help. You're the chairman, the celebrity, the one with nationwide political and social influence. I'm not even a French citizen. I'm honored to be asked, but I'm sure whatever you want can be easily achieved without me. Still, thank you again for being so kind as to ask."

"No, no, Mrs. Villers!" stammered Celine taking her longtime rival's left hand earnestly with both entreating, own. "I'm absolutely serious! There's a big favor—I need from you. It's a favor you alone are capable of providing. A favor I fully understand and appreciate you won't be expecting of me too"

She paused before holding her guest's hand firmer in an uncharacteristic show of personal friendship. "Given we've never precisely been—*chums*–it's even better this way. It will be seen as a—"

"Pardon me, Countess? I don't follow?"

"Don't mind me. I'm just a *Scatterbrains*," apologized Celine. "Even someone as *educated* as you couldn't possibly sort out the *Witless Woman* nonsense I so frequently prattle, Mrs. Villers."

"Don't speak that way of yourself!" the mathematician swiftly intervened, her voice protective. "Please stop speaking in that demeaning way of yourself, Countess! I've differed with you often over the years we've been on the garden trust board together. But it wasn't once because I ever thought you a *Scatterbrains* or judged your opinions *nonsense*!

It's exactly because you're not a *Scatterbrains* and the proposals you make on which we differ are anything but *nonsense* that I feel I must so strongly express a contrary view!"

She paused.

"And please don't call me Mrs. Villers anymore. Call me: *Ashraf*."

"On the condition you please address me as *Celine*."

"If you wish, Celine.*"

"So I do, Ashraf"

They pecked lips.

Embraced.

The seeming impenetrable, unbridgeable chasm separating the pair abruptly closed. Unaware both *Messalina* and the *Angry Woman* possessed this gentle, empathetic, vulnerable, affectionate private side, each, was delighted at her discovery. Each was filled with a vast, unmitigated appreciation for what she'd found. The ladies now wished desperately learning as much as possible about the mysterious, endearing stranger each knew both so well and not, at all.

"You can't imagine what this all means to me, Ashraf!" bubbled Celine. She'd wished to voice something more profound but, in the end, decided simple words were no less illustrative of her innermost thoughts.

"I'm doing no more than speaking the truth!" bubbled Miss Kermanshani, now adopting an intimate, confidential voice. "Anyway, more times than you can imagine, I've agreed with you completely. It's only because the others on the board follow you like sheep that I felt obliged for the sake of democracy to stand in opposition. We're, after all, the *Ladies Garden Trust*, not the Soviet *Politburo.*"

"Ah! If only I realized, Ashraf!"

"Well, you do now, Celine!"

They pecked lips.

Embraced.

"As I told you earlier, life does have its surprises, Ashraf."

"But please tell me what this–*big favor*–only I'm able to grant, is, Celine?"

"I wish you to succeed me as leader of the garden board," revealed its present chairman, she at last remembering the reason why the two ladies came together this morning. "I know that, like me, you've got a lot of other personal commitments. However, no one else can better lead this board—can better see to the maintenance of the garden as well as–you, Ashraf."

"Are you sure, Celine?"

"Indeed I am, Ashraf. I intend to continue on the board, and I'm sure we'll still have our differences at times. But so be it. I'm confident in my friend's leadership. As you said, this is the *Ladies Garden Trust*, not the Soviet *Politburo*. A vote in opposition on certain matters is also helpful for democracy."

They pecked lips.

Embraced.

Two souls become one.

SCHERZO

NEWS OF THE FORMAL ENGAGEMENT of Marie-Agnes-Ferdinande de Godefroy, elder daughter of Countess Marie-Therese-Celine de Montfort to Jacques-Claude-Maurice de Polignac Duc d'Aveyron: president of the *World Bank*, he soon also to become secretary-general of the *United Nations,* ignited furious speculation throughout French Monarchists circles since the Second World War was this wealthy, exclusivist, self-perpetuating social elite as transfixed on a single issue. It, as intrigued not only with the upcoming nuptial but its possible long-term national and international consequences. As the wedding day neared, refined, genteel royalist tongues of both sexes wagged elegantly almost nonstop.

"Is a truly historical crossroads at hand?"

"Or, a great positive change afoot?"

"Is an older, finer cultural epoch on fast return?"

"Does the engagement signify that following its long eclipse, monarchism is again ascendant?"

All members of this still politically ambitious yet socially influential tribe were eager to discover the much-yearned truth. Each heatedly debated the undisclosed guest list. Which wealthy grandee and his fashion-plate wife or high-maintenance mistress was granted the matchless privilege of attending the wedding? And even more titillating for social rivals *of both sexes*—who was *not* so privileged.

Interest in young courtesan Ferdinande de Godefroy's journey to the altar was not restricted to monarchist circles, however. The plans for this illustrious ceremony, its long-term social and political repercussions, the names on and *off* the fabled guest-list—were all topics of no less compelling discussion among office-seekers, financiers, movie and television producers, diplomats, dress designers, milliners, feminists,

Caterers; charity fundraisers, public relations firms, urban planners, legitimate journalists, gossip-columnists, "experts," talking-heads, entertainers, hoteliers, career civil servants, even nuns, and clergymen. All unanimously agreed that Mama's engineering of her elder daughter's marriage to the Duc d'Aveyron, was Countess de Montfort's "greatest triumph yet."

God save the Queen!

God Save Queen Celine!

Our one true and noble Queen!

If royalists, business groups, and upper-middle-class opinion-makers were intrigued by the affair, Countess de Montfort's corps following— the General Public—was *enraptured.* For the tens of millions of urban blue-collar workers, shopkeepers, farm laborers, university students, housewives, teenagers, clerical staff, lonely romantics, old movie lovers, unrecognized talents, and dreamy little girls for whom Countess de Montfort provided vicarious fulfillment of their frustrated-hopes, the triumph of "Our Celine" was a victory all might forever cherish. To those mobbing her on the street, begging for and duly receiving her kind advice, baptizing their children with heroine's name, "Our Celine" was to each and all, a close, personal friend.

So touched was she upon receiving a bouquet of fresh, fragrant white roses from shy little girl Jeannette that "Our Celine" promptly arranged for the child to attend the wedding service seated atop the grand lady's own protective lap.

God save Queen Celine!

I

The portentous day at last arrived.

"I'm ever-so immensely-pleased you could attend with me, Ashraf-sweetheart!" pledged Celine, wearing a fine, tailored, not-off-the-rack, light pink outfit as she and her no less fetching companion exited St. Severin, the famous, tan and brown *Romanesque* Left Bank church at conclusion of Ferdinande de Godefroy's nuptials. The Duke and his new Duchess having already departed for the wedding reception in a separate vehicle, the Mother of the Bride and her own special chum traveled to the event in another sleek, shiny, black, feline, stretch-limousine. This automobile was chauffeured by the *Good Little Soldier's* hero: adventurer, spymaster Brigadier Aslan.

"Oh! I wouldn't miss your daughter's wedding for all the world, Celine-sweetheart!" replied Ashraf, clad in a fine, tailored, not-off-the-rack, turquoise outfit. She began to readjust the angle of her wide, John Singer Sargent-reminiscent chapeau. "I'm so honored to be invited simply, honey! I so-hope the new Duchesse d'Aveyron likes the gift I bought for her."

"Don't trouble yourself, Ashraf, dear! I know that my daughter Ferdinande—you and I had better start to get accustomed to addressing her as—*Your Grace*—will be delighted with your splendid gift!" chirped Celine.

"Wait! Wait! Just a moment," interjected the Countess, breaking her thought. "I'll do it for you, Dear."

"Oh, but of course," responded the Mathematician, accepting loyally as if to the truth of a well-established scientific formula. "You know how to get it correct."

Celine proceeded to readjust further the angle of her chum's wide, John Singer Sargent-Edith Wharton-reminiscent chapeau. The international hoopla created by her offspring's decision to marry and choose the bridegroom in no way diminished Mama's continued absolute, unchallengeable authority to dictate the style, shape, size, and even manner of wearing feminine headgear.

"There. That's much better."

"Thank you, Celine."

"In addition, Ashraf sweetheart," the Countess de Montfort illuminated, bubbling, "you were the very first I thought to invite! The ceremony would never be as wonderful as it was without you, my best buddy, sitting at my side!"

"I love you, Celine!"

"I love you, Ashraf!"

Each woman's body conveyed a timeless, delicate, vulnerable fragrance.

Friends embraced.

Pecked lips.

Two yearning souls briefly become one.

Following their protracted years of bitter rivalry, long mutual-suspicion, Countess de Montfort and Mrs. Villers, now her successor as chairman of the *Ladies Garden Trust,* never once failed to address each other in "Tu" intimate **Second Person Familiar**.

II

Since the duo's momentous confrontation at cream color No. 3 Rue Artemis, once seeming intractable-foes were transformed into near-inseparable chums. The Louvre, Sainte Chapelle, Notre Dame, the Carnavelet, Eiffel Tower, the Trocadero, Invalides, the Luxembourg Gardens, and all the other marvelous artistic and historical sites of Paris these cherished friends now always insisted on visiting together.

"I love you, Celine!"

"I love you, Ashraf!"

Upon climbing down from Montmartre to the river embankment, the devoted comrades leisurely strolled or merrily skipped along the Seine hand-in-hand, jabbering-away. The two, often exploding into furious laughs as if they were affectionate, giddy teenage girls on vacation from convent school.

"I love you, Ashraf!"

"I love you, Celine!"

On several weekends, the Pianist took the Mathematician to stay with her at the spacious Seventeenth-Century Montfort country estate in Berry. Once, so that she might demonstrate her skill at flying a *Huey* helicopter, the unschooled Countess also took her *Educated* chum to spend quality time at the family residence at Mount St. Anne. Located over seven thousand feet above sea level in the French Alps, domed by clear, aquamarine sky, the chateau, in addition, contained its mistress's personal collection of Brueghel, Holbein, Clouet, and Claude Lorain paintings.

"You're a true Renaissance-*Lady,* Celine-sweetheart!" exclaimed the Iranian-American expatriate. She was deeply impressed by the art collection to be found in her exceptional pal's mountain hideaway. "This could be a museum! I really mean it! The Montfort Museum! You're gifted at so many different, no-less intriguing, thought-provoking things! I only wish we could have become close friends far earlier."

"Well, we are close friends now, Ashraf-sweetheart! Today and forever, the best and most loyal of friends!" replied the Countess almost touched, moved. "And I am so glad, so delighted, honored, overjoyed you no longer consider me just a *Scatterbrained Female.*"

"No, no!" entreated Mrs. Villers, waving her own sculpted arms to provide emphasis. "You are certainly not *Scatterbrained Female.* It was *Witless. Scatterbrains* of me to ever imagine it so! No, no, Celine-sweetheart. You are a true Renaissance-*Lady!*"

"Say, Love?" queried Ashraf moments later, she at last unable to resist asking a question on her mind since the duo's first private encounter. "That Manet at your home in Paris! I thought I saw that one in a museum.'

"Oh, you mean dear *Olympia* was keeping us regal company in the salon!" giggled Celine with rightful pride. She was delighted at an opportunity to divulge the true story.

"Like Michelangelo's *David* standing in the public square in Florence, Italy, the Manet painting visitors see in the Musée d'Orsay is just a copy. The original *Olympia* is found at No. 3 Rue Artemis! Manet and my ancestor Countess Isabelle de Montfort who is posing for the famous nude, were intimate friends. The artist left the original version of the masterpiece with her."

But please, please," begged Celine, "never tell the press or the tourists!

"I promise, my dear heart!"

"Bless you, Ashraf, my so many-faceted darling!"

Considering the intense camaraderie, a keen friendship developed between the former-*Messilina* and erstwhile-*Angry Woman.* It was only natural that this jolly pair should be seen skipping from St. Severin Church hand in hand after Ferdinande de Godefroy's marriage ceremony. After that, they were later climbing into the black, shiny, feline, stretch limousine. Celine and Ashraf were driven to the wedding reception held at the splendid, sprawling, Seventeenth-Century Palais Aveyron located in the 16th Arrondissement on the western suburban edge of Paris. To uninformed observers, these two fetching ladies possessed an emotional bond forged in their earliest childhood.

A PAINFUL REMINDER

"SOME OF THE OTHERS INVITED to the reception are purely the Duc d'Aveyron's political and business associates," explained Celine to her chum as the Montfort land dreadnaught entered the spacious, manicured palace grounds; next, arrived at the chateau's weeping front marble staircase; where a valet in Eighteenth-Century livery stepped up to open the car door so that its two dainty passengers might emerge. "I know some of these other individuals only by name, photograph, or reputation."

"Well, I'm sure they are all the most charming, engrossing of people," replied Ashraf, debarking from the massive vehicle as a cultivated lady is trained. "In his profession, during his international sojourns, the Duc d'Aveyron must come across the most intriguing sort of individuals."

"Yes, Ashraf, so he does!" agreed Celine, easily mistaken as *a sister,* not *the mother* of the Bride.

Click, click, click, click, click by two pair of comradely high heels.

The dedicated buddies walked up the weeping front neoclassical marble staircase and were then shown into the palatial residence. Passing through a long *Rococo* hallway flanked by vintage Gobelin tapestries and Houdon busts atop marble pedestals, the ceiling high above decorated with Tiepolo and Watteau frescoes, this fetching, fragrant twosome, at last, joined the crowded reception held in a large *Louis XV Style* salon. The spacious chamber possessed: a dark, hardwood, waxed floor under *Safavid Dynasty* carpets; Greuze, Boucher and Chardin paintings; red, green, blue damask *Queen Anne* furniture.

Click, click, click, click, click.

Suddenly, catching sight of one individual amid the crowd, Ashraf gasped.

Her body froze in place.

She turned deathly pale.

When at last she able to reopen her mouth, Ashraf could only mumble, stammer. Her brown eyes, usually, so perceptive, lively, now stared at the figure ahead in helpless, abject terror.

"Whatever is wrong, Sweetheart?" asked Celine, alarmed. "It's him!" companion stammered. "*Him*!" Slowly, furtively, Ashraf pointed ahead.

Mrs. Villers gestured toward a certain individual found among a group of fashionable-attired ladies and dapper gents. He was seen chatting, drink in hand at the center of the salon. "Him! *Him*!"

"Oh yes, Ashraf, the professor–the professor. Like you, he's from America. Quite a notable chap too, he is, or so I've been told. He just received the Nobel Prize in Mathematics. He came up with some splendid new theories, equations. Don't ask me ever to try explain them–math is hopelessly over my own poor *Witless Woman's* head. Obviously, though, his discovery was significant enough to be awarded a Nobel Prize."

"Yes, indeed."

Do you possibly know him, Ashraf?" ventured Celine, detecting a previous and not satisfactory connection between the two academics. "Were you once his student, his friend, his colleague, or acquaintance? Would you like me to introduce you to him?"

Her worried friend made no reply.

Instead, Ashraf remained frozen in place, her brown eyes projecting helpless, abject terror.

If he also discomfited by their abrupt, unexpected reunion, Dr. James Hardwick betrayed no sign. Rather, he manifested kindness, graciousness, chivalry itself. A wide smile on his face, his outstretched right hand offering courteous welcome, he stepped forward to greet the two pretty ladies.

"It appears my friend Mrs. Villers knows you from somewhere before, Monsieur," observed Celine, accepting the greeter's hand. "Was

Mrs. Villers once a student of yours back in America? Was she perhaps once a colleague, a neighbor, perchance?"

"No, I am afraid we've never met before, Countess de Montfort," answered Dr. Hardwick with a straight face, exhibiting no sign or gesture of unease. "Perhaps your friend Mrs. Villers is mistaking me for someone else."

Following several moments of anxious silence, another well-healed, snappy-clad gent summoned from across the crowded, elegant room. Showing no interest in continuing the present conversation, Dr. Hardwick instantly obeyed, walked away. "Pardon me ladies, duty calls."

"Let me get out of here!" begged Ashraf, her power of proper speech at last returned. "I must get out of here *fast,* Celine! Give my humblest, most effusive apologies to your sweet, charming daughter Ferdinande. Please assure Ferdinande I'll make up for my hasty, rude departure many-many-many-times-over later in the week. However, I absolutely just can't stay here now a second longer!"

She fled.

ADAGIO

"AMAZING! SPLENDID! AWESOME! I DIDN'T know this about you, too!" exclaimed Celine, ever-so intrigued with her friend's newest revelation. She was deeply honored at discovering herself to be the very first person in all Europe privileged to be entrusted with the great secret. "You're such a fascinating, remarkable creature! Or, as my daughters would say: *you're awesome!'"*

"Thank you so much, Celine," responded Ashraf, short of breath, her heart and lungs pounding. "I hope I'm worthy of your kind words."

"Of course you are, Sweetheart! Now, please, please. Show me more."

"As you wish, Celine."

The two ladies were seated upon adjoining cherry wood damask chairs inside the study of Mrs. Robertson Villers' spacious apartment in the 7th Arrondissement. Along three broad walls were bookshelves crammed from floor to sixteen-foot ceiling with often-read distinguished books and frequently consulted valuable United States, British, French, and German scholarly periodicals. On the fourth wall, beneath an oriel window looking out upon the flowering Luxembourg Gardens, was a large, multipurpose oak secretary. Its desk was covered with piles of letters, newspaper cuttings, learned magazines, and manila envelopes postmarked from celebrated academic institutes in both Europe and the United States. Found here also was a *Mackintosh* computer, a printing machine, a telephone, and yet additional bound and unbound learned publications. Atop the room's dark-stained, the hardwood floor was laid a colorful, intricately designed Persian rug.

"Just a moment, Celine."

As the Countess de Montfort, wearing a parakeet blue outfit, looked on, her lively green feminine eyes registering deep admiration, Mrs.

Villers, clad in a canary yellow outfit, rose to her feet, unlocked a lower drawer of the secretary, and after a furious search, at last, brought out a battered, battleship-gray tin box.

Today was the morning following the two friends' unexpected encounter with Dr. Hardwick at the Palais d'Aveyron.

"Don't over-exert yourself, Ashraf honey," pleaded Celine, crossing her pretty legs opposite. "We have the whole rest of the day to study the document. I can stay as long as it takes for you to show me."

"Yes, yes, here we are, Celine!" announced her expatriate Iranian-American buddy at last, triumphant. She is now returning to her seat, then taking several moments to catch a breath. "Here, we are!"

As she opened the tin box to reveal its sacred, long-hidden contents, Ashraf enjoyed a priceless rush of innocent, unmedddled with girlish enthusiasm. A sensation she'd not felt since those heady days at university.

"Show me, Ashraf, show me!" entreated Celine, clapping with similar virginal glee, her own body to experiencing a priceless rush of innocent, unmeddled with adolescent exuberance.

Both virgins crossed their pretty legs opposite, same.

Hem of each one's short dress, receding, like.

"Here we go, Celine. I've got them all saved, all still kept in order."

"Ooh! What a brainy little *Thing* you are, Ashraf, honey!"

"Thank you."

Atop a small coffee table just beside, Mrs. Villers assembled a series of dogeared college writing pads. Every lined page of the tablets was covered with the former-grad student's own intricate handwritten notes, her elaborate mathematical formulas, and complex personal geometric diagrams. Next, the one-time faculty mascot brought forward a stack of distinguished scientific journals, each one containing a different prize-winning article authored by a certain *Miss Ashraf Kermanshani, a doctoral candidate at X University.* Finally set on the table was the famous periodical containing the monograph presented to the international academic community by Dr. James Hardwick.

Large sections of this latter documents were either underlined in his protegee's red handwriting or marked with references to this sidekick's own published articles.

"And they always say: **'girls aren't good at math!**'" giggled Celine, upon surveying the impressive scholarly material. "And they always say **girls aren't good at math**!"

"Whoever the all-powerful, whoever the all-knowledgeable supreme, omnipotent–*they*–are!" commented Ashraf.

Celine crossed her pretty legs, opposite Hem of short dress receding.

"You sound just like my younger child, Rolande," laughed her mother, fondly. "'Don't be so worried about those dreadful–*they* people, Mama,' *Missy* tells me. ‹If *they* are really so smart, really so accomplished, really so gifted–then those characters should also have the courage to show their faces! **They** should let their voices be heard–not instead always prefer fleeing into the shadows–always wishing to be known simply as the great amorphous– *they*. Don't be scared, Mama. Don't be frightened of the big, bad **they**. '"

After a moment of reflection, Rolande's mother added: "In the last few months, Mama has tried her feeble best journey *Missy's* path."

She pecked Ashraf on the lips tender, pressed her right hand affectionately.

"It looks Celine as if your family and mine possess much more in common than one might initially think!" observed the former-*Angry Woman* to erstwhile-*Messalina*

"Quite so!"

On the wall to the right were hung a Berthe Morisot, André Derain, and Marie Laurencin.

"But please, please!" urged Celine, gesturing to the papers atop the coffee table. Each scientific equation, mathematical formula she saw recorded was as magnificent, superb in its seeming-simple, apparent-effortless beauty as the historic loops, spins, twirls, and jumps of Golbihar Kermanshani's never to be equaled three consecutive gold-medal-winning Olympic figure skating performances. "Please, please, tell me more about your research, about your discoveries!"

Ashraf proceeded to describe her triumph and betrayal at the university. She recounted how after devising some of recent history's most critical mathematical theories, she then found the credit brutally snatched away, shamelessly awarded to others. Others, she long purported to be her friends, her protectors, mentors. After first hailing Ashraf as the golden child of Mathematics, as Academia's brightest young star, these men abruptly turned on their gifted young protegee, expropriating her finest, most valued work as their own. They, forever destroying the girl's career and reputation in America, denouncing Ashraf to the national press as a heartless Delilah, Jezebel, as a scheming, fanatical Iranian terrorist.

"Oh, you so ill-used noble sweetheart–you, so tragic, misunderstood dear!" consoled Celine at the conclusion of the tragic tale. Her voice was breaking, eyes teary, she reached out to hold her gifted companion close. "If I'd only learned of this terrible business, this awful miscarriage of justice earlier!"

"It would have done no good," replied Ashraf. "I was little more than a child then. I was very immature. I was absolutely in no position to confront the media circus exploding around me after I denounced the professor. Having until then lived only either at home under my father's strict supervision or within a cloistered, intellectual ivory tower, I was in no condition to successfully take on the bigger world's nasty, self-seeking hubbub!"

She reflected.

"Finally, I lost my nerve. I panicked. I rushed over to Golbihar's house. I ran to my room. I locked the door behind me, climbed into bed, pulled the covers over my head, and just waited for the storm to pass."

"You so poor, unfortunate dear!"

"Unable to reverse the outcome," continued Ashraf, "humiliated, blackballed, any prospect for a university career gone, I tried as best as I could forget, pretend it all never happened. I left the state. I got married. I took my husband's name. I bore him a child. Mr. Villers was a kind, courtly, refined, older, Australian gentleman. I allowed him to protect, shield, make all the decisions and provide for me. I regarded myself more as his daughter than his wife."

On the wall to the left hung the nude portrait of Ashraf by David Hockney.

"I know all this sounds dreadfully old-fashion," the Mathematician acknowledged, "but for a time, being *old fashion,* being protected, being shielded, provided for, letting a strong man make all the decisions, was precisely what I needed. It worked. I did forget the pain. Then, following so good, sweet Mr. Villers' death, I moved to Paris. Thinking I was now safe, thinking the notorious ‹Miss Kermanshani' was now forever left on the far side of the ocean, I started publishing articles once more, again delivering speeches."

Ashraf clenched her jaws, eyes, and hands.

"Then yesterday," she said, "at your daughter Ferdinande's wedding reception when I thought all was getting better–that man suddenly reappeared!"

"Dr. Hardwick?"

"Yes, Celine, Dr. Hardwick."

"The professor who just won the Nobel Prize?"

"Yes, Dr. Hardwick, who just won the Nobel Prize–*my N*obel Prize."

Outside, sparkled the Luxembourg Gardens.

Trees rustled, merry.

Flowerbeds smiled in welcoming bloom.

In all directions, a riot of vibrant, splendid colors.

The most luscious shades of blue, red, white, yellow, green, orange, violet.

Birds took flight.

Children scampered.

Nannies chatted.

Elderly gentlemen with memorable stories to tell, played cards and chess.

"Are these your only copies, Ashraf, dear?" queried Celine after a thoughtful moment. She gestured to the documents atop a coffee table.

"No, honey. I left duplicates on a floppy disc with Golbihar back in Amherst, Massachusetts. However, those you see on the table are the only copies in my possession."

"Well, then I must go home and get my photographic instruments, Ashraf, you so ill-used, you so-exploited, you so misunderstood noble Sweetheart," responded Celine eagerly. "I must now put all these papers on tape unless they're lost or stolen."

She rose to feet, headed for the door, a committed, resolved look on her pretty face.

"Some grand moguls of public opinion have long owed me a favor!" explained Celine. "It's now time I get them to pay me back."

ROLLING THUNDER

AS BECAME ABUNDANTLY CLEAR THE next morning at news kiosks throughout France and all her present and former colonial possessions, Countess de Montfort was as good as her genteel word.

THE GREAT NOBEL PRIZE ROBBERY cried one mass distribution daily.

FAMOUS EXPERT ONLY LIAR shouted second huge national journal

HIGHEST AWARD FOR PLAGIARISM chimed in, the paper of record.

HARDWICK IS FRAUD thundered, a fourth popular news outlet.

HARDWICK, A COLLABORATOR warned no less best-selling, fifth.

Soon, from Berlin: Philippine Luria, from London: Léonie Golitsyn, each loyally added her own dainty *Montfort Ladies* share to raising a concerted media cackle. A furor originating in the morning print press of France quickly proliferated across national borders. It is soon capturing the wrapped-interest–both justified and voyeuristic–of AP, AFP, BBC, Reuters, Al Jazeera wire services, of newspapers, magazines, television stations, *Facebook, Twitter, Instagram.* The juicy tale is also seizing the imagination of populist call-in radio talk shows, religious evangelists, pamphleteers, soapbox orators, tee-shirt, and poster-makers; pop-singers, stand-up comics throughout Europe, North America, Africa, Japan, and Asia.

Professor James Hardwick suddenly found his portrait removed from the cover of several prestigious academic periodicals. He was soon dropped from requests to deliver university commencement addresses. He failed to receive invitations to top-money speaking engagements, was abruptly removed from television talking-head panels and was passed over for membership on blue-ribbon government commissions. In Stockholm, the normally so-gracious King and Queen of Sweden, who always invited each Nobel Prize winner to the palace for an intimate, private dinner before presenting the historic award, chose not to extend their welcome to this years' Mathematics winner.

While the Nobel Prize cannot be taken away or transferred to others, the validity, the significance of its original receipt is always open to criticism, reevaluation. Although Celine's girlfriend never attained the public recognition she deserved, the thief certainly did not escape with his ill-gotten-gains, unscathed.

Higher Mathematics' celebrated *Hardwick Laws* are now forever marked in scientific journals and college textbooks with an asterisk. (*Many contend these essential pillars of modern science were actually formulated by Ashraf Kermanshani of Tabriz, Iran).

If today, she in large measure the worldly figure tutored by pragmatic Auntie Bernarde, her friendship with Ashraf demonstrates that in spirit, Celine remains the daughter of romantic Countess Manon. While outwardly the seductive political manipulator portrayed in newspaper cartoons, Celine is still at heart Brigadier Aslan's *Good Little Soldier*.

"Follow, my Mama, follow Countess Manon's, example, *Treasure*," whispered Celine upon receiving the letter announcing Rolande's flight from President Markovsky's garden party. "Be heroic like Mama! Take up the challenge like my Brigadier! Succeed, and you'll become the greatest Montfort Lady of them all!"

www.ingramcontent.com/pod-product-compliance
Lightning Source LLC
Chambersburg PA
CBHW050456110726
47899CB00003B/968